PENGUIN P

TEN WHITE

Gerbrand Bakker won the Internation
for his first novel, *The Twin*. He work
before becoming a gardener. He lives

David Colmer is the translator of G
winning novel, *The Twin*.

International Acclaim for
Gerbrand Bakker and *Ten White Geese*

"A beautiful, oddly moving work of fiction, a quiet read that lingers long in the mind, like the ghosts that linger in our homes, and in the land around us . . . Assured and mature . . . Even more powerful [than *The Twin*]."   —John Burnside, *The Guardian* (London)

"Simple and devastating . . . Written and translated with lapidary precision, perspective, and crisp prose; there is emotion and expression, but held back from the writing, which is controlled and full of clean, physical detail."   —*The Independent* (London)

"A novel full of hints and mysteries [that] will almost certainly keep you rooted to your chair until the dénouement."
—*The Spectator* (London)

"Bakker's writing is fabulously clear, so clear that each sentence leaves a rippling wake."   —*Los Angeles Times*

"A beautiful, convincing, subdued novel [with] a spare simplicity and expressiveness reminiscent of J. M. Coetzee."
—*Trouw* (The Netherlands)

"Intensely moving . . . An incredibly tender book, capturing new and old relationships in simple yet beautiful detail."
—*The Tattooed Book* (UK)

"With his fine style and gripping plot twists, this is a writer who ultimately grabs his readers by the throat."   —*Nederlands Letterenfonds*

"Bakker sees beauty and complexity in the smallest corners of everyday life and portrays them with a quiet mastery."
—*The Quarterly Conversation*

"Bakker is the best writer of nature in the Netherlands. How he writes about geese, reeds, and grassy paths through a meadow makes me weep. I imprisoned myself with the story, pulled up the blankets and wanted to disappear into it. This book is a beauty."
—Marleen Janssen, Libell.nl (The Netherlands)

"An accomplished work [with] many clear parallels [to J. M. Coetzee]: both authors dish out their novels in spare, economic prose and manage the trick of skirting on the surface of their characters whilst hinting at great storms of emotion underneath." —*Booktrust* (London)

"The type of book you need to read in a single evening. Then you're gradually hypnotized by the calmly and sharply observed story."
—*De Standaard* (Belgium)

"Gripping . . . Thrillingly fresh . . . It bears his indelible poetic stamp, his incisor cut. . . . Galvanizing." —*Irish Independent*

"An enchanting style by a wonderful writer. He knows how to evoke a lot of tension with minimal resources."
—*Tros Nieuwsshow* (The Netherlands)

"Mesmerizing . . . So spare and so poignant . . . haunting and charismatic . . . It is impossible to put it down without feeling a deep sense of acquaintance with its wild, neglected terrain, and with the foibles and aspirations of his characters. . . . Highly recommended."
—*The Age* (Melbourne, Australia)

"This novel proves that great literature benefits from a simple setting." —Literatuurplein.nl (The Netherlands)

"Monumental." —*Titel Magazin* (Germany)

"You do not want to miss this!"—*Linda Magazine* (The Netherlands)

"Tranquility and tension generate a quiet triumph."
—*Sunday Business Post* (Ireland)

"Captivating. It is all deceptively straightforward. But this makes the turns in the story much more surprising and thrilling."
—*Nederlands Dagblad*

"Through his reserved storytelling Bakker creates the enormous poetic force that he has made his own."
—*Neue Zürcher Zeitung* (Switzerland)

"Phenomenal. There is no other word for Gerbrand Bakker's new novel." —*Noorhollands Dagblad*

"Confirm[s] Bakker as a leading light of new European fiction."
—*Wales Arts Review*

"Terribly gripping . . . there is a continuous tension, a tension only the very best of thrillers have." —*Kurier* (Austria)

Ten White Geese

A NOVEL

Gerbrand Bakker

TRANSLATED FROM THE DUTCH
BY
David Colmer

PENGUIN BOOKS

PENGUIN BOOKS

Published by the Penguin Group

Penguin Group (USA) Inc., 375 Hudson Street, New York, New York 10014, USA
Penguin Group (Canada), 90 Eglinton Avenue East, Suite 700,
Toronto, Ontario M4P 2Y3, Canada (a division of Pearson Penguin Canada Inc.)
Penguin Books Ltd, 80 Strand, London WC2R 0RL, England
Penguin Ireland, 25 St Stephen's Green, Dublin 2, Ireland (a division of Penguin Books Ltd)
Penguin Group (Australia), 707 Collins Street, Melbourne, Victoria 3008, Australia
(a division of Pearson Australia Group Pty Ltd)
Penguin Books India Pvt Ltd, 11 Community Centre,
Panchsheel Park, New Delhi–110 017, India
Penguin Group (NZ), 67 Apollo Drive, Rosedale, Auckland 0632,
New Zealand (a division of Pearson New Zealand Ltd)
Penguin Books (South Africa), Rosebank Office Park,
181 Jan Smuts Avenue, Parktown North 2193, South Africa
Penguin China, B7 Jiaming Center, 27 East Third Ring Road North,
Chaoyang District, Beijing 100020, China

Penguin Books Ltd, Registered Offices:
80 Strand, London WC2R 0RL, England

First published with the title *De omweg* by Uitgeverij Cossee 2010
Published in Great Britain by Harvill Secker 2012
Published in Penguin Books 2013

1 3 5 7 9 10 8 6 4 2

Copyright © Gerbrand Bakker and Uitgeverij Cossee, 2010
English translation copyright © David Colmer, 2012
All rights reserved

ISBN 978-0-14-312267-8
CIP data available

Printed in the United States of America

Ample make this bed.
Make this bed with awe;
In it wait till judgment break
Excellent and fair.

Be its mattress straight,
Be its pillow round;
Let no sunrise' yellow noise
Interrupt this ground.

Emily Dickinson

November

1

Early one morning she saw the badgers. They were near the stone circle she had discovered a few days earlier and wanted to see at dawn. She had always thought of them as peaceful, shy and somehow lumbering animals, but they were fighting and hissing. When they noticed her they ambled off into the flowering gorse. There was a smell of coconut in the air. She walked back along the path you could find only by looking into the distance, a path whose existence she had surmised from rusty kissing gates, rotten stiles and the odd post with a symbol presumably meant to represent a hiker. The grass was untrodden.

November. Windless and damp. She was happy about the badgers, satisfied to know they were at the stone circle whether she went there or not. Beside the grassy path stood ancient trees covered with coarse, light grey lichen, their branches brittle. Brittle yet tenacious, still in leaf. The trees were remarkably green for the time of year. The weather was often grey. The sea was close by; when she looked out from the upstairs windows in the daytime she occasionally spotted it. On other days it was nowhere in sight. Just trees, mainly oaks, sometimes light brown cows looking at her, inquisitive and indifferent at once.

At night she heard water; a stream ran past the house. Now and then she would wake with a start. The wind had turned or picked up and the rushing of the stream no longer carried. She had been there about three weeks. Long enough to wake up because a sound was missing.

2

Of the ten fat white geese in the field next to the drive, only seven were left a couple of weeks later. All she found of the other three were feathers and one orange foot. The remaining birds stood by impassively and ate the grass. She couldn't think of any predator other than a fox, but she wouldn't have been surprised to hear that there were wolves or even bears in the area. She felt that she was to blame for the geese being eaten, that she was responsible for their survival.

'Drive' was a flattering word for the winding dirt track, about a kilometre and a half long and patched here and there with a load of crushed brick or broken roof tiles. The land along the drive – meadows, bog, woods – belonged to the house, but she still hadn't worked out just how it slotted together, mainly because it was hilly. The goose field, at least, was fenced neatly with barbed wire. It didn't save them. Once, someone had dug them three ponds, each a little lower than the last and all three fed by the same invisible spring. Once, a wooden hut had stood next to those ponds: now it was little more than a capsized roof with a sagging bench in front of it.

The house faced away from the drive towards the stone

circle (out of sight) and, much farther, the sea. The countryside fell away very gradually and all of the main windows looked out over it. At the back there were just two small windows, one in the large bedroom and one in the bathroom. The stream was on the kitchen side of the house. In the living room, where she kept the light on almost all day, there was a large wood-burning stove. The stairs were an open construction against a side wall, directly opposite the front door, the top half of which was a thick pane of glass. Upstairs, two bedrooms and an enormous bathroom with an old claw-foot tub. The former pigsty – which could never have held more than three large pigs at once – was now a shed containing a good supply of firewood and all kinds of abandoned junk. Under it, a large cellar, whose purpose she hadn't quite fathomed. It was tidy and well made, the walls finished with some kind of clay. A horizontal strip window next to the concrete stairs offered a little light. The cellar could be sealed with a trapdoor which, by the look of it, hadn't been lowered for quite some time. She was gradually expanding the area she moved in; the stone circle couldn't have been much more than two kilometres away.

3

The area around the house. She had driven to Bangor once to do the shopping but after that she went to Caernarfon, which was closer. Bangor was tiny but still much too busy for her. They had a university there and that meant students. She had no desire to set eyes on another university student, especially not a first year. Bangor was out. In the even smaller town of Caernarfon, a lot of the shops were closed, with *FOR SALE* daubed on the windows in white paint. She noticed shopkeepers visiting each other to keep their spirits up with coffee and cigarettes. The castle was as desolate as an outdoor swimming pool in January. The Tesco's was large and spacious and open till nine. She still couldn't get used to the narrow, sunken lanes: braking for every bend, panicking about left or right.

She slept in the small bedroom on a mattress on the floor. There was a fireplace, as in the large bedroom, but so far she hadn't used it. She should have really, if only to see if the chimney drew. It was a lot less damp than she'd expected. Her favourite place upstairs was the landing, with its L-shaped wooden balustrade, worn floorboards and window seat. Now and then, at night, sitting on the window seat and looking out into the darkness through the tendrils of an old creeper, she would notice that she wasn't entirely alone: somewhere in the distance there was a light. Anglesey was in that direction too and from Anglesey you could catch a ferry to Ireland. The ferry put out to sea at fixed times and at other fixed times it put into harbour. Once she saw the sea gleaming in the moonlight, the water pale and smooth. Sometimes she heard honking from the goose field, muffled by the thick walls. She couldn't do anything about it; she couldn't stop a fox in the night.

4

One day her uncle had walked into the pond, the pond in the large front garden of the hotel he worked at. The water refused to come up any higher than his hips. Other staff members pulled him out, gave him a pair of dry trousers and sat him on a chair in the warm kitchen (it was mid-November). Clean socks were not available. They put his shoes on an oven. That was about it, or what she knew of it anyway, no one ever went into any more detail. Just that he'd walked into the pond and stood there a while, wet up to his hotel-uniform belt. Surprised, perhaps. He must have judged the water to be deeper.

Her being here had something to do with that uncle. At least, she had begun to suspect as much. Scarcely a day passed without her thinking of him, seeing him before her in the smooth water of the hotel pond. So far gone that he hardly realised that hip-deep water wasn't enough to drown in. Incapable of simply toppling over. All of the pockets of the clothes he was wearing stuffed with the heaviest objects he had been able to find in the hotel kitchen.

She hadn't thought about him for a very long time. Perhaps she did now, in this foreign country, because it was November here too or because she sensed how vulnerable people are when they have no idea what to do next, how to move forward or back. That a shallow hotel pond can feel like a standstill, like marking time with the bank – no start or end, a circle – as the past, present and unlimited future. And because of that, she also thought she understood him just standing there and not trying to get his head underwater. A standstill. Without any form of physicality: no sex, no eroticism, no sense of expectation. In the few weeks she'd been in the house, with the exception of when she was in the claw-foot bath, she had not once felt any impulse to put a hand between her legs. She inhabited this house the way he'd stood in that pond.

5

She had set up the large bedroom as a study. More precisely, she had pushed the worm-eaten oak table that was there when she arrived over to the window and put a desk lamp on it. Next to the lamp she placed an ashtray and next to the ashtray she laid the *Collected Poems of Emily Dickinson*. Before sitting down at the table she usually slid the window up a little. When she smoked, she blew the smoke at the crack. In this room the leaves of the creeper annoyed her, so one day she took the rickety wooden stepladder from the pigsty and hacked the tendrils in front of the window away with a knife. That gave her an unimpeded view of the oaks, the fields and – very occasionally – the sea, and left her free to think about what the word 'study' still meant to her, if anything. Behind her was a divan she'd made her own by covering it with a moss-green cloth. She had stacked a few books on a small table next to it, but didn't read a word. She'd put the portrait of Dickinson in the exact middle of the mantelpiece, in a Blokker picture frame. It was the controversial portrait, a copy of the daguerreotype that had been listed for sale on eBay.

Sometimes the light brown cows stood at the stone wall that separated the fields from her yard; they seemed to know exactly which window she was observing them from. *My yard*. I could do something with that, she thought, smoking one cigarette after another. She wondered which farmer the cows belonged to, where his farmhouse was. These hills brimming with streams and brooks and copses were much too complicated and confusing for her. Now and then she laid a hand on the Dickinson, running her fingers over the roses on the cover. She bought a pair of secateurs and a pruning saw at a hardware shop in Caernarfon.

6

She took the house as it was. There were a few pieces of furniture, a fridge and a freezer. She bought some rugs (all the rooms had the same bare, wide floorboards) and cushions. Kitchen utensils, saucepans, plates, a kettle. Candles. Two standard lamps. She kept the wood-burning stove in the living room going all day. The kitchen was heated by a typically British cooker that burnt oil from a tank squeezed between the side wall and the stream and hidden from view by a clump of bamboo. The enormous contraption doubled as a water heater. The day she moved in she found hand-written instructions on the kitchen table with a flat stone as a paperweight. Whoever wrote them signed off by wishing her *Good luck!* She wondered very briefly who it could be, but soon dismissed it as irrelevant. She followed the instructions on the piece of paper exactly, step by step, and wasn't really surprised when it fired up. That night she was able to fill the large bath with steaming-hot water.

It was just those geese; they were peculiar. Had she rented the geese too? And one morning a large flock of black sheep suddenly appeared in the field beside the road, every one with a white blaze and a long white-tipped tail. On *her* land. Who did *they* belong to?

7

She discovered that the path that led to the stone circle – and went on beyond it, though she'd never been farther – joined her drive where it bent sharply. A kissing gate in a thicket of squat oaks was completely overgrown with ivy. By the look of it, nobody had been through it for years. On the far side of the gate was a field with long, brown grass. There had to be a house somewhere; a chicken coop with a dim light that burnt day and night stood a bit farther down the drive. She cut away the ivy with her new secateurs and sawed off the thick stems close to the ground. The gate still worked. She found an old-fashioned oil can in the pigsty and oiled the hinges. Only then did she realise that the path followed her drive, then crossed her yard before passing through a second kissing gate in the low stone wall and leading across the fields to the wooden bridge over the stream. A *public footpath*, apparently, and she had a vague recollection of that being something British landowners couldn't do much about. With the hinges oiled, she walked to the road with the oil can still in her hand and turned right. After a couple of hundred metres she found the sign with the hiker, his legs overgrown with lichen. She didn't dare climb over the stile, scared as she was of coming out at the house she still hadn't seen. It was the first time she'd turned right. Caernarfon was to the left. She walked a little farther, the sunken road rising slightly. After about ten minutes she reached a T-junction and there she saw the mountain for the first time and realised what a vast land-scape existed behind her house and how small an area she had moved in until that moment. All at once, she became aware of the oil can in her hand. She rubbed a blister on the inside of her thumb and quickly turned back. The geese honked loudly at her, as they had every time she'd walked past. The next day she bought an Ordnance Survey map at an outdoor shop in Caernarfon. Scale: 1–25,000.

8

On a cold night she decided to test the small fireplace in her bedroom. She had to open the window. Not to let out smoke, but heat. Even with it open, the room was so hot she had to lie naked on top of the duvet. And instead of thinking about her uncle, she saw the student, the first year. She parted her legs and imagined that her hands were his hands. After a while she turned on the light, not the main one, but the reading lamp on the floor next to the mattress. Her breasts looked monstrous on the white wall, his hands even larger. It was as if the burning wood was sucking all the oxygen out of the small room; she couldn't help but pant. Although there were no neighbours, she kept seeing the dark uncurtained window and herself lying there. Aroused woman alone, fantasising about things long past, things she would be better off forgetting. That unspoilt body, lean and lithe, the powerful arse, the hollows behind the clavicles, the jutting pelvis. The selfishness, the energy and thoughtlessness. Anyone who cared to could look in through the uncovered glass, at least if they took the trouble to lean a ladder against the wall and push aside a few of the creeper's tendrils. Afterwards she smoked a cigarette in the study, still naked. She saw herself sitting there, shivering in the cold. She blew smoke up over her face and thought about him sitting in front of her later, among the other students, one of many, with the face of a sulking child. A spiteful egotistical child, and as ruthless as children can be.

9

The next day the sun was shining. The weather here was nothing like she'd expected; it could be very still and quite warm, even now, deep into the year. Around noon she went to the stone circle. The badgers weren't there. That didn't strike her as strange, almost certain as she was that they were nocturnal. On the detailed map she'd bought she had found a green dotted line running up her drive and across her yard. It even gave the name of her house. The house that belonged to the chicken coop turned out to be less than a kilometre away; there were several farmhouses in the immediate vicinity. The stone circle was indicated by a kind of flower with *stone circle* written next to it in an old-fashioned font. The mountain was Mount Snowdon. At the stone circle she felt like someone was watching her, whereas before it had been almost as if she had discovered it. She took off her clothes and lay on the largest boulder like a cold-blooded animal. It warmed her back. She fell asleep.

For a few nights now the rushing stream no longer calmed her: noises – creaking boards, the shuffling of what she hoped were small animals, and an almost unbearably plaintive cry from the woods – kept her awake, and awake she started thinking. She got wound up again, defiant and angry.

She sighed and tossed and turned, imagining what was happening to her body. She also tried to localise the mild, nagging pain. Nagging and not, as she had expected, gnawing: like dozens of tiny beaks slowly but surely eating their way through her insides. Maybe she just responded well to the paracetamol she was taking. She grew anxious too. Last night, looking at herself smoking, she saw her face change into a stranger's: a voyeur rather than a reflection. It was November; in December the days would be even shorter. *Curtains*, she had written on the piece of paper lying on the table in front of her. It was the first word she wrote down. She went back to the bedroom, closed the window and lay there gazing at the bare glass for quite a while, her heart pounding as if she'd been running up and down the stairs.

When she first woke she didn't understand what was happening down at her feet. She thought of the wind and gorse bushes. Whatever it was touching the soles of her feet, it wasn't sharp. Very carefully she raised her head from the stone. First she saw a white stripe, a stripe through black patches to either side of it – she immediately thought of the heads of the black sheep. Small dark eyes peered up from between her feet. The badger was staring straight at her groin. Her neck muscles started to quiver, her forehead pricked beneath her hair. The animal looked at her and she wondered if it could really see her, if a badger understood that eyes were eyes. It was as motionless as she was, but with the vertebrae at the top of her back pressing painfully against the stone that wouldn't last much longer. Then the animal began to climb slowly up onto the rock, between her calves and knees. It raised and turned its head and started sniffing, nose slanted, looking straight ahead. She shot up, moving both hands to cover her groin and shocking the badger so much it jumped, half turning in mid-air in an attempt to get away. It landed on her left leg, her foot blocked its escape route and it bit into her instep. She had time to grab a branch up off the ground and swung it, bringing it down hard on the badger's back, so hard it snapped with a dry sound that made her gasp, despite the fright, and think, Oh God, I hope I haven't crippled him. The badger writhed and growled and lurched off under a gorse bush. A few birds took flight. After that it became very quiet again. Blood ran down her foot and dripped onto the stone, but it didn't hurt too much and she thought, Let it bleed for now. She lay down again. The stone no longer gave off any warmth. She let one hand rest on her groin; her body seemed to have come back to her. Strange that she hadn't realised that last night. And peculiar that she automatically thought of an animal that attacked her as 'him'.

Lacking a first-aid kit, she cut up an old T-shirt, quarter filled the bath and soaked her foot in the hot water until the skin was wrinkled. Then she tied a strip of material around it. Later she pulled *The Wind in the Willows* out of the pile of books on the small table next to the divan and rediscovered how gruff and solitary badgers can be, an animal that 'simply hates society'. That night her foot started to throb.

10

She had left her mobile phone lying there in the cabin weeks before when the ferry docked punctually in Hull, so the best she could come up with now was to drive to the tourist information centre in Caernarfon to ask about a doctor. Driving was difficult. Her foot was swollen, she couldn't get it into a shoe. Pulling on a pair of jeans proved equally impossible and that was why she was wearing a skirt. Letting out the clutch, the pedal felt as hard as a rock, hard and rough. Veils of thin rain passed over the windscreen. She thought of the stove in the living room and wondered if she should have put it out. And she worried that the last GP might have left Caernarfon, that it would say *FOR SALE* on his window too. The helpful tourist ladies would send her on to Bangor.

'Holiday?' the doctor asked.

'No, I live here,' she said.

'German?'

'Dutch.'

'So what's the matter with you?' The doctor was a thin man with yellow hair. He was sitting there smoking away in his surgery.

'May I also smoke?' she asked.

'You may. We all have to die of something.'

While lighting up, she thought about the inadequacy of English personal pronouns. This man's 'you' sounded informal to her, whereas the woman at the tourist information counter had said it in a more formal way, like a Dutch '*u*'. Listeners had to decide for themselves how they were being addressed and respond accordingly. She drew hard on her cigarette to clear the rising image of the first-year student.

'Your foot?'

'Yes. How do you know that?'

'I saw you walk in. There was a degree of difficulty. And most people who come through that door wear two shoes.'

'I was bitten by a badger.'

'Impossible.' The doctor stubbed out his cigarette.

'But I was.'

'Liar.'

She looked at the man. He really meant it.

'Badgers are meek animals.' *Meek?*

'Are you religious?' she asked.

He pointed to a cross on the wall next to a crooked poster warning against HIV infection: an obscure shape she couldn't quite place and the words *Exit only*.

'And yes, one day there will be nothing but badgers walking around this town. People have already started to move away. Badgers and foxes. Or they just up and die, that's an option too of course. Could you perhaps tell me how you possibly came to be bitten by such a meek animal?'

Not enough personal pronouns and an excess of round-about verb constructions, she thought. 'I was asleep.'

'Did the animal get into your house? Do you live here in town?'

'I live up the road. I was outside, lying on a big rock.'

'Did the badger bite you through your shoe?'

'Do you have time for all this talk? I'd rather you look at my foot.'

'It's quiet this morning. You sound a little hoarse. Trouble with your throat?'

Hoarse? Did she sound hoarse? 'Maybe I have a temperature.'

'Are you tired too?'

'Dead tired. But that –'

'You weren't wearing any shoes?'

'Yes. I mean, I'd taken off my shoes.'

The doctor looked at her, but let it slide. 'Show me.' He gestured at a bed.

She hopped over and struggled up onto it, as it was quite high. She pulled the thick sock off her injured foot.

'Ouch,' the doctor said.

'Yes,' she said. 'It's damn painful.'

He took her left foot and squeezed it cautiously. Then he ran a hand up her shin. 'There are scratches here too,' he said.

She tried to restrain the blush rising from her throat, but knew how pointless that was. 'Yes,' she said simply.

'The badger?'

'Yes.'

He rubbed her knee. 'Not just the shoes.'

'The sun is still very strong here even in November,' she said.

'We have a marvellous climate.'

She sighed.

'Any other complaints?'

Before answering, she glanced around the surgery once again. 'No.'

'Are you sure?'

'Why do you ask that?'

'People don't come here for a splinter in their eye. They use it as an excuse to casually mention all their aches and pains.'

She kept her eyes on the cross. Like the poster, it was slightly crooked. The doctor finally took his hand off her knee.

'If you're sure it was a badger, I'll need to give you a tetanus injection.'

'It was a badger.'

'I'll leave the wound. Soak it two or three times a day in hot water with a couple of teaspoons of baking soda dissolved in it. It's an old remedy. And I'll put you on antibiotics.'

The injection hurt like hell. After throwing away the phial and needle, he immediately lit up a fresh cigarette. With the cigarette in the corner of his mouth and one eye watering, he wrote out the prescription. 'Do you know where the chemist is?'

'No,' she said.

'Six houses along.' He looked at his watch. 'He's open now.'

She stood up and accepted the prescription. 'Thank you.'

'If the wound's no better after about four days, come back.'

'I will.'

'And watch out for badgers.'

'Yes.'

'Badgers and foxes. Foxes have a nasty bite on them too.'

'They're too busy with my geese,' she said.

The doctor started to cough.

My geese, she thought on the way to the chemist's. Now they're my geese all of a sudden. Hopping was too difficult: she could hang the sock in front of the stove at home and if she wore a hole in it, she could throw it away. A young couple were walking towards her, laughing and talking loudly, arms around each other's waists. When they passed her, the girl looked at her as only girls who think the world is theirs for the taking can, lost in the happiness of the moment and insisting on making others party to their bliss. It was almost offensive: unadulterated happiness that would very soon come undone. Share my joy! the girl beamed. She met her gaze with indifference, ignoring the boy. Having young women half her age walking around at all was unbearable enough. Seconds later she pushed open the door to the chemist's. There was no queue at the counter.

Along with the antibiotics she had been prescribed, she bought a full first-aid kit, five boxes of paracetamol, hand cream, a tube of toothpaste and a couple of tubes of cough drops. 'Holidays?' the woman behind the counter asked.

'No,' she said.

'German?'

'No.'

'Sore foot?'

'Yes.'

The chemist's assistant completed the transaction in silence.

It was still raining. She drove back to the house at a snail's pace.

11

That evening she could hardly move her arm and her foot was still throbbing. She boiled some potatoes, then fried them up with a couple of onions and five cloves of garlic. Two glasses of wine with dinner. She felt like drinking more but remembered hearing that alcohol and antibiotics were a bad combination. The doctor hadn't mentioned it. No surprise there, he was too busy smoking himself to death in a surgery with a cross on the wall. After dinner she climbed the stairs like an old woman, a weak hand on the banister and dragging her leg. There was still a little light coming in through the two windows and she lay down on the divan in the study. Flowers, she thought. This room needs flowers. A phone would be handy too. A badger had bitten her on the foot – she could have broken both her legs. The doctor hadn't said anything about a stiff arm either. A radio. It was so quiet she could hear the individual sheets of rain passing the windows and, between them, the bamboo scraping against the oil tank at the side of the house.

She smoked a cigarette.

She lay there. *The heartless bitch.*

It was 18 November.

12

The husband had been past every noticeboard in the English Department. In a blind spot on the wall between two offices, he had found another note half hidden behind a list of exam results. It was exactly the same as the one in his hand. *Our 'respected' Translation Studies Lecturer screws around. She is in no way like her beloved Emily Dickinson: she is a <u>heartless</u> Bitch.* He realised that the same message must have hung on a lot of boards. He walked to her office. It was very quiet in the long, narrow corridors of the university building. On the door, under his wife's name and the name of a colleague he *had* heard of, there was a new plastic plate with a man's name and the title: Lecturer, Translation Studies. He hesitated, finding it hard to imagine they'd already cleared away all her stuff. Computer, books, notes – surely they'd still be here? As far as he knew she was no longer employed as a lecturer, but maybe they still let her work on her thesis in the office. He went in; there was no one there. Shortly afterwards he came back out into the corridor and started shouting. Two men put out the fire with a hose on a reel, managing to contain it to this one office. When the fire brigade arrived ten minutes later, there was nothing for them to do. The husband waited calmly for the police to show up.

*

The note was lying on the table in the interview room of the nearest police station. He had already admitted arson and had pulled the note out of his back pocket halfway through questioning. 'I'll break his neck,' he said.

'That's not allowed,' said the policeman who was taking his statement.

'Then I'll cut his dick off.'

'That's definitely not allowed.' The policeman asked him where his wife was at that moment.

'I don't know. She's gone. That's all. In her car, and the trailer's not in the shed any more either.'

Did that leave him without transport?

'No. We had two cars.'

Had he tried to contact her?

'What do you think? Of course I have! Her mobile phone just gives the engaged signal the whole time.'

Were things missing from the house?

'All her clothes and a coffee table, a hideous thing actually, I'm glad to be rid of it. A mattress, duvets. Lamps! And all kinds of odds and ends. Books, quite a bit of bedding, a portrait of Emily Dickinson –'

'Who?'

'She's an American poet. She was writing about her, doing a PhD thesis. Bit late, if you ask me, but she obviously had something to prove. Christ almighty.'

Did they have kids?

That was the only time the husband looked down.

What was the state of their relationship?

'What's it to you? What am I doing here anyway?'

The policeman reminded him that he had committed an act of arson in a university building.

'So what! Just do your job and keep out of my private life.'

The policeman ended up by asking him whether he wanted to register his absent wife as a missing person.

The husband raised his head. 'No,' he said after a long pause for thought. 'No, let's not do that.'

Would he like some coffee?

He looked at the policeman. 'Yes,' he said. 'Thanks.' While he was drinking the coffee, the policeman waited patiently, a friendly expression on his face. Then the husband said, 'A single.'

'What?'

'The mattress she took was a single.'

13

She lived in constant expectation of a visitor showing up. Those geese belonged to someone, so did the black sheep along the road. Someone would come eventually, if only a lost hiker. The idea filled her with restlessness. After a few days her foot stopped throbbing and she could see the wound contracting. When it was drying off after the soda bath, she would run her thumb over the itchy teeth marks for minutes at a time, even though she had hardly dared look at it immediately after the bite. Along with the incompatibility of alcohol and antibiotics, she also remembered hearing that you had to complete a course of treatment, and continued taking the tablets. Her upper arm, which was still stiff, now bothered her more than her foot. It kept raining, but it was gentle rain; she didn't even put on a coat to go out. One Sunday she heard a few shrieking whistles, from which direction she found it impossible to determine. She got out the map and discovered a railway line not far away, the Welsh Highland Railway. Next to Caernarfon there was a picture of an old-fashioned steam engine. Evidently it ran at weekends.

14

Several days after the other staff members pulled him out of the pond, her uncle started to make a cabinet. It was actually more of a wall unit. 'See,' her mother told her father, who was the uncle's brother. 'See. That's how you do it. You do things. You get on and do them.' He spent weeks on it, weeks of leave, as the hotel management had told him to come back when he was 'feeling better'. Sawing, drilling, screwing, sanding, painting; sitting on a chair and staring at what he'd done so far. When he finished, he had a slight relapse. 'I wouldn't have put it past him to take the whole thing apart again,' her mother said. 'But he didn't.'

15

She had bought the secateurs and the pruning saw on impulse because she wanted to do something about the creeper clinging to the front of the house. Cutting back the ivy had been enjoyable. She gazed out through the glass in the front door at the grass rectangle between the stream and the low stone wall the light brown cows sometimes gathered behind. Along the stream were a few overgrown shrubs and some strangely shaped trees. Right in front of the house, the grass ended at a wide, ragged-edged gravel path. No, it wasn't gravel, she saw when she stepped outside and knelt down for the first time. It was pieces of slate, and she realised that the grey mound behind the house wasn't just a grey mound, it was a supply of crushed slate. She rubbed her left upper arm and went back into the house to put on her oldest trousers. In the bathroom she pushed two paracetamol out of a strip and washed them down with a mouthful of water.

In the pigsty she found a rusty spade and an even rustier pitchfork. She leant them against the low wall, placing the secateurs on top of it. The veils of rain faded into mist, as if a cloud had sunk to the ground. She sighed. From a number of spots along the front wall of the house, she took five steps forward and set a piece of firewood on the ground: one log ended up on the crushed slate, the others on grass. After sticking the spade into the ground and trying to push it down with her good foot, she immediately gave up. It was pointless, she needed clogs. Clogs and a wheelbarrow, cord and short stakes. She put the spade back against the wall. There was a strong smell of cow dung. I have to look carefully and think it through, she thought. That's all it takes. If I wanted to – really wanted to – I could even put a wall unit together. Jobs like that go step by step. For now, the work was done. She took the secateurs and walked around to the side of the house, where some of the bamboo almost reached the roof. She cut it off at shoulder height and, half an hour later, glancing at the pile of bamboo behind her, realised she could cross the stakes off the list. She had uncovered a small window she hadn't noticed inside, in the kitchen. Since coming outside she hadn't smoked a single cigarette. Now she would find it difficult to get her right hand up to her mouth.

Later that day the cloud rose and the sun broke through. She walked slowly to the stone circle with the secateurs in her hand, cutting off branches that were in the way and removing ivy from the iron kissing gates. The path was looking more and more like a real path. After reaching the stone circle and before sitting down on the largest rock, she carried on in the same direction and came to a stile. It was wet here, really wet, marshy. With thick clumps of coarse grass sticking up between small puddles. The path led straight through the bog on a kind of natural embankment with rocks dotted here and there. Tomorrow, she thought. On the map she had seen a larger body of water, rectangular, as if it were man-made.

She sat dead still, waiting, her arms around her raised knees. No badgers appeared. Two yellow butterflies fluttered over the gorse. Two butterflies, she thought. *Two butterflies went out at noon, / And waltzed above a stream.* An enormous wave of homesickness washed over her. She had felt a milder version a couple of times before in the enormous Tesco's at Caernarfon, especially in the refrigerated aisles. She'd fought it, but here in the sun with the butterflies and the gorse, the memory of the street in De Pijp was impossible to resist. She saw it before her in black and white: the trees half as big as now, cars with rounded features and bodies, children in knitted cardigans with leather patches on the knees of their trousers, the steep stairs up to the front doors, the heady smell of St Martin's sweets – St Martin's Day! Just over a week ago. She released her knees and stretched her legs, hugged her belly and bent forward.

Shortly after that, the badger shuffled out from under its gorse bush.

16

When she got back from the stone circle with an armful of tufted grass, there was a piece of paper on the front door. *Came round, nobody home. I'll be back, maybe tomorrow. Rhys Jones.* The note was stuck on with a piece of chewing gum.

She turned to look at what would be the garden. I can't do this, she thought. I don't even know what those shrubs are called. I don't know who Rhys Jones is. How can I protect seven geese from a fox? She dropped the secateurs and the bundle of grass. The sun was already low. *Presentiment is that long shadow on the lawn, / Indicative that suns go down; / The notice to the startled grass / That darkness is about to pass.* Dickinson had seen what she saw now. The homesickness had ebbed. She walked into the living room, poured a glass of red wine, fluffed up some cushions and sat down close to the wood-burning stove. The cigarette she lit tasted like a first cigarette. It grew dark very slowly, as if the light was being sucked out of the window like fine dust. It made her feel a little dizzy. She lit a couple of candles and put three logs in the stove. She had left everything behind, everything except the poems. They would have to see her through. She forgot to eat.

17

The next morning she stumbled over the bundle of grass. Swearing, she put it in a big glass vase she found in a kitchen cupboard. She left the secateurs lying on the ground. Then she hitched the trailer to the back of the car and drove off in a random direction. This was the UK, she'd be bound to run into a garden centre sooner or later. After about an hour she found herself in a village called Waunfawr. There was no garden centre, but there was a bakery. She bought bread, biscuits and a cream cake. She didn't have a clue where she was, even though the mountain she saw in the distance when she entered the shop looked familiar. To be on the safe side, she told the baker the name of her house.

'Don't you know where you are?' he asked.

'No,' she answered.

The baker didn't say anything, he just shook his head gently.

'I have a poor sense of direction.'

The baker looked out at the car parked directly in front of the shop. 'Start the car, drive straight ahead, follow the road, turn left after a mile, then left again.'

'So close?'

'So close. And from now on buy bread here.'

'Pardon?'

'From now on buy bread here. Now that you know where we are.'

'Of course.'

'We're open Sunday mornings too.' He turned to an open door. 'Awen!'

The baker's wife stuck her head round the corner.

'A new customer. She lives in old Mrs Evans's house.'

'Oh, nice,' said the baker's wife. 'Hello, love.' She disappeared again.

'Thanks.' She walked to the shop door. 'Do you also know of a garden centre in the area perhaps?'

'Bangor. Know where that is?'

'Yes.'

'Good.'

'See you later.'

'When you run out of bread.'

'Yes.'

'German?'

'No, not at all.' She walked out of the shop and put her purchases on the back seat of the car. She looked around. A few houses, hills, a crossroads. Not even Mount Snowdon was enough for her to get her bearings. '*Godverdomme*,' she said to the mountain. 'I'll have to go home first.' The baker had taken up position at his shop window and was standing with one arm stretched out like a signpost. The only part of him moving was his hand which, with a pointing index finger, was jerking up and down like a wind-up toy. She nodded, turned her collar up a little to conceal the hot patches on her throat and quickly climbed into the car.

She turned onto the drive and noticed immediately that the field was empty. It was only after taking the sharp curve that she saw the black sheep a good deal nearer the house. The seven geese were gabbling close together. She braked and got out. Six. She counted them again, even though they were close to the fence, and again she got no further than six. If it carries on at this rate, she thought, there'll be none left by Christmas.

The piece of paper was gone from the front door, replaced with a new message. *Called again. I moved my sheep. I'll try again. Tomorrow morning at 9. Rhys Jones.* Fine, she thought bravely. A sheep farmer and a time. I've got a cake.

She picked up the secateurs and went into the kitchen. The map was still spread out on the table; she no longer folded it up. She located Waunfawr. Incredibly close by. She stood there like that for a moment with her back bent, both hands flat on the map. After a while, the green dotted lines showing the walking paths all seemed to converge on her drive, on her land. That mountain, she thought, I have to keep an eye on Mount Snowdon, then I'll know where I am.

18

That afternoon she didn't just buy a wheelbarrow, cord and garden clogs. She also loaded a roll of chicken wire, a hammer and nails onto her trailer. There weren't any students at Dickson's Garden Centre, but there were elderly women and retired men with happy grandchildren, customers clutching long scrawled lists, who left nothing to chance. Soft classical music led them down the aisles. Babbling fountains and water features were equally soothing. She stayed longer than necessary, ordering a cup of coffee at the Coffee Corner, taking a second look at the roses and buying three flowering indoor plants, the kind her grandparents had on their windowsill thirty years earlier. She also bought a better pair of secateurs; the ones from the hardware shop were already loose and blunt. A gawky kid with red curls helped her hoist the wheelbarrow up onto the trailer. When she was about to get into the car, he held out a hand for her to shake. She couldn't think of anything better to say than, 'Thank you. That was very friendly of you.' The boy didn't say a word, he just grinned and shut the car door. In the wing mirror she saw him watching attentively as she drove off.

*

That afternoon she let the new garden rest, using the wheelbarrow to transport the chicken wire to the three ponds instead. The six geese were standing waiting for her. When she walked through the gate and into the field, they ran off. As if they're expecting something from me, she thought. But what? She used one foot – the injured one, to test it – to push against different parts of the collapsed hut. After she had pulled away a few planks, the roof, which was covered with tarred sheets, rested on the ground as a triangle. More than enough room for the geese. She unrolled the chicken wire and realised that she would need something to cut it. As before, she found useful tools in the old pigsty. She walked back up the drive with a saw, a large pair of pincers and a roll of thin wire. First she closed off the back of the triangular shelter, fixing the chicken wire in place by nailing it tight under planks that weren't completely rotten. Look carefully and think it through, she thought. If I do that, I could even put together a wall unit. Clucking quietly, the geese watched her. In the next field the black sheep had come closer and most of them were now lined up at the fence. She pulled the packet of cigarettes out of her coat pocket and lit one. A big bird, brownish red, swooped down into the boggy copse and landed on a branch of an oak, facing towards her. 'Is it you?' she called out in English, as if a bird wouldn't understand her if she spoke Dutch. It stared at her unmoved. She threw the half-smoked cigarette into one of the ponds.

She did the front differently, first cutting planks to size, then using them to close off the top of the triangle. She left wide gaps between the planks; there wasn't enough solid wood. The chicken wire was 120 centimetres wide. Again she walked back to the pigsty, this time to look for staples. She found them too. She lined the wire up along the ground, folded the superfluous triangle down over one side of the roof, then attached it by pounding staples in with the hammer. Then she didn't have a clue. She took a few steps back and considered the shelter. She looked at it and thought deeply. She felt like giving up. Everything in her body said: Stop it. Leave it. Go inside, have a drink, smoke a cigarette, lower your body into a bath full of hot water. There were two good planks left. The short one standing up and the long one on the ground, she thought, and after that I can work out how to close off that last bit of chicken wire, which has to serve as a kind of door. Just keep at it. After nailing the two planks to each other at right angles with another piece of wood at an angle as a brace, she put the structure up against the front of the shelter, then crawled inside to staple the wire to the wood. With nothing to hold the horizontal plank in place, it was very difficult to get them in. 'Godverdomme,' she said. She had to put something behind the plank. She crept back out of the shelter and looked around. There were large rocks by the ponds. Much too heavy. The wheelbarrow, upside down. She pushed it up hard against the plank and tried again. The wheelbarrow started to slide away, but by hammering as lightly as she could, she managed to get the staples into the wood anyway. Her arm hurt, she could feel her foot. Cursing, she crawled back out of the shelter, wondering what in the name of God she was doing. She pulled the wheelbarrow out of the way, turned it upright and checked her handiwork. It seemed reasonably solid. Solid enough, she thought, to keep out a fox. A big bird definitely couldn't get in. Now she just had to figure out how to close off the last bit without nailing it shut permanently. She had about ten large nails left and pounded six into the roof at intervals of about twenty centimetres, exactly opposite the triangle she'd stapled down on the other side of the roof. She cut lengths of wire and twisted them to attach them to the chicken wire, also at twenty-centimetre intervals. She made sure the lengths of wire were more or less aligned with the six nails and only then did she trim off the excess chicken wire. '*Godverdomme!*' she said again. She stank of goose shit and her hands were bleeding.

The geese refused to be herded into the shelter. They ran off the wrong way in a column or scattered, as if understanding that it was hard to choose between six separate birds. The sheep in the adjoining field remained unmoved. Most of them grazed on calmly; some looked up now and then. Panting, she scooped up a few pebbles and threw them at the geese. 'Ungrateful, dirty, filthy, stinking, pig-headed creatures!' she shouted. 'I'm trying to bloody save you!' She decided to try again one last time, very calmly. The geese were standing by the largest pond, close to the shelter. She lit a cigarette and sat down in the grass. The geese clucked a little, two of them drank some water. Not too fast, she told herself, I'll let them get used to me first. She stood up and spread her arms, cigarette in mouth. Taking their time, the geese thronged away from the pond and walked past the shelter. She stayed where she was. The birds stopped four or five metres away from the bent piece of chicken wire. 'Go inside,' she said quietly. 'Go on. It's safe in there.' She listened to herself speaking English and thought, I have to head them off. Very calmly. As quietly as she could, she crept around behind the geese, believing she was going to succeed: the birds stood still with their fat bodies pressed against each other, only their heads and necks turning. Now she walked towards the shelter, arms still spread. Yes, she thought. Yes. Smoke curled up into her eyes, making tears run down her cheeks.

In that same instant something skimmed over her head, so close she felt the wind rustling her hair. A half-second later, the reddish-brown bird flapped its wings, then glided up over the house and off into the wood. By that time the geese were already in the far corner of the field. A few white feathers floated down to the ground. She fell to her knees and collapsed sideways in the wet grass. 'Why am I doing this?' she said quietly. She spat out what was left of the cigarette. 'I can't do it at all.'

A couple of hours later she was lying in the claw-foot tub. She studied her fingers, raised her left leg and picked the scab off her instep. The water at the foot of the bath took on a reddish tinge. 'I *can* do it,' she said. She got out of the bath and dried herself. The small mirror above the sink was misted over; she saw her face and upper body as pinkish lumps and took a couple of paracetamol. She draped the towel over the rail on the landing next to some damp clothes. A fire was burning in the fireplace in the study, the desk lamp on the oak table was switched on. She stood in front of the fire. The skin of her thighs and belly felt tight. She ran her hands over her breasts and looked Emily Dickinson straight in her black eyes. 'It's easy for you,' she said. 'You're dead.'

19

It wasn't until a couple of days after she'd abandoned her mobile phone on the ferry that she realised she'd always used it as a watch and calender. She had brought her diary with her; if she really wanted to she could work out the date. Not having a clock – the one on the kitchen wall had probably stopped a long time ago – was not a problem. She ate when she was hungry and went to bed when she was up to it, though never without taking a paracetamol first. No alarm clock.

When she came downstairs the next morning, she was able to walk straight out the front door, which was wide open. It was already light and the grass was damp on her bare feet. *These are the days when skies put on / The old, old sophistries of June, – / A blue and gold mistake.* She wasn't entirely sure why those lines had popped into her head. November and still so mild. Deceptively mild, perhaps. Blue and gold, but a mistake. There were two rubber boots on the doorstep. She turned round and didn't close the door. The man was sitting at the kitchen table as if he came for a coffee every morning. He had folded up the map and was calmly drumming his fingers.

'*Bore da,*' he said.

'What time is it?' she asked.

He gestured over his shoulder with a thumb.

She looked at the clock: thirteen minutes past nine. She couldn't remember what time it had been stopped at all these weeks.

'Have you been here for a quarter of an hour?'

'Yes.'

All she had on was the baggy T-shirt she used as a nightie. It came down to just above her knees. Was it too late to go back upstairs?

The man stood up and extended a hand. 'Rhys Jones.'

If he hadn't stood up, she could have excused herself. She pulled the neck of the T-shirt up a little and held out her other hand. 'Good morning,' she said without giving her name. She filled the coffee pot with water and coffee and raised one of the lids on the big cooker. She heard the farmer sit down again, the chair creaked.

'Indestructible, that is,' he said.

She looked out of the window. 'Milk?' she asked, keeping her back to him.

'Yes, please. Milk and sugar.'

She raised the second lid, took a plastic milk bottle out of the fridge and poured the milk into a small saucepan. She picked the whisk out of the cutlery tray, which was on the worktop. She saw that her hand was shaking. 'I'm just going upstairs,' she said, not budging.

The man didn't react.

'I'm going to get dressed. I overslept.'

'You don't need to on my account,' said Rhys Jones.

She faced him. 'Wasn't the door locked?'

He reached into his back pocket and pulled out a key, which he laid on the map. 'I have a key.'

'Which you are now leaving here?'

'If you'd rather.'

'Yes, I'd rather.' She turned away again to stir the milk with the whisk, feeling her bum rocking slightly beneath the thin T-shirt material. 'There is cake. Would you like a piece of cake with your coffee?'

'Lovely.'

The coffee pot started to splutter. 'Did you write the instructions?'

'Yes.'

'You did it very well then. I can manage the Aga now.'

'The oil tank's been filled. It'll last you months.' He slid the map to one side. 'Mrs Evans liked the idea of me having a key.'

She poured the coffee into two mugs and added milk to one. Then took the cake out of the fridge, cut two slices and laid them on plates. She slid the cake and coffee over to him and, before sitting down and as inconspicuously as possible, held the hem of her T-shirt against her thighs.

Rhys Jones looked like a caricature of a Welshman: a broad face, thick greasy hair, watery eyes, unshaven. She thought she could detect a faint smell of sheep, but it could have been last night's beer. The nail of his right thumb was blue and torn. He finished the piece of cake in five bites.

'You've been down with the geese,' he said.

'What was the arrangement you had with the woman who lived here before?'

'Regarding the sheep?'

'Yes.'

'Free pasture. Mowing and haymaking once or twice a year. And a lamb in autumn.'

'A lamb?'

'Butchered.'

'And that lamb? I get that too?'

'That's right. You're living here now. My sheep are grazing the land you're renting. The arrangement's the same.'

'And if I don't like lamb?'

'You still get it. I can't supply pork or beef, but the lamb is excellent.' He stared at her. 'Zwartbles.'

'Pardon?'

'They're Zwartbles sheep, a Friesian breed. From your own country.'

She looked at her cake and knew she wasn't going to eat it. Never again would she see this man at nine o'clock in the morning, she thought. 'Was this Mrs Evans a relation of yours?'

'No.'

'Why wasn't the house sold?'

'She had no one. I asked an estate agent friend of mine to put it up for rent.'

'To make sure you can still graze your sheep here?'

'Amongst other things.' He slurped what was left of the coffee out of his mug. 'Meanwhile they're looking for family. It could take a while.'

'Another?' she asked.

'Lovely.' He relaxed a little on his chair and stretched his legs out under the table. 'I arranged her funeral.'

'Are the geese yours too?'

'No. They belonged to Mrs Evans.'

'So now they're mine?'

'Yes. More or less.'

She had to stand up to get his mug and walk over to the sink with it. He stared at her as if he knew how difficult her situation was. 'More or less,' she said. 'What does that mean?'

'They're rental geese. They don't belong to you. I'd be guessing you're not allowed to put a rented goose in the oven for Christmas roast.'

She stood up, staring back at him so that he wouldn't be tempted to lower his gaze. It worked, he didn't glance down at her hips until he had handed her his mug. She put the milk pan back on the hotplate and stared outside again, where the grass now looked a little drier. She wished she was out there: digging with the spade, stringing the cord along the path, working on a metaphorical wall unit. She noticed that the three flowering plants on the windowsill needed watering. She was appallingly tired and got a numb feeling in her arm while whisking the milk. But a numb arm was nowhere near as bad as talking to a man who had apparently come to assert his authority over the land and this house.

'I only counted six by the way.'

'What?'

'Six geese.'

'Have you been counting my geese?'

'Of course.'

Goddomme, she thought.

'Mrs Evans looked after them well. She fed them bread.'

She refilled the mug with coffee and milk and calculated how long it would take him to drink it. She no longer cared what he thought of her and, after passing him the mug, even bunched the T-shirt up a little to sit down. He started drinking straight away, sliding the key back and forth across the hard cover of the map with his free hand. She pushed away the cake and didn't say another word.

'It's a temporary situation. The house is occupied. You're happy, I'm happy, the agent's happy. But the situation can change at any time.' He bent forwards and pulled her plate over. 'May I?'

She didn't answer, but he ate her slice of cake all the same. It disgusted her, the broken thumbnail hovering round his chewing mouth. Silently she watched him gulp down the coffee. Then she stood up. She didn't know what to say. Maybe he'd work out for himself that he'd spent long enough sitting in her kitchen. She gestured at the living room and the front door.

'Aye, I'm on my way again,' he said. He rose and walked slowly to the living room. 'Easy,' he said. 'Having all the furniture, like.'

'Why isn't there a bed?'

'I took it.'

'And the clock?'

'Climbing up on a stepladder was completely beyond her. I used to change the battery every now and then.'

She was pleased to see him crossing the room in his socks. A man in socks, and especially a man in socks with holes in them, is hard to take seriously.

At the front door he turned and looked her over from head to toe. 'Injured?' he asked.

'Bitten by a badger.'

'Impossible.'

'I still got bitten.'

'Badgers are shy animals.' *Shy*. He stepped over the threshold. 'I'll be back then,' he said, before pulling the door shut behind him.

He doesn't want me to see him bending to pull on his boots, she thought, and smiled. 'Goodbye,' she called through the door when she saw that he was reaching down. She dragged herself upstairs and lay on the divan in the study, closing her eyes. Rhys Jones tore off in his car, which was undoubtedly green. A pickup, probably, with room for a few sheep in the back. Or bales of hay. A double bed. She didn't feel the slightest inclination to look out of the window. Two hours later she started the day again. Properly, this time.

20

The sun was shining and the grass had dried completely. There was almost no wind. She cut the bamboo poles down to bamboo posts and stuck them in the ground next to the pieces of firewood. She strung cord between the posts. The light brown cows stood in line watching her over the stone wall. The grassy field was at least half a metre higher than the field the cows were in; on their side the wall was much taller. They snorted. With her mind more or less a blank, she used the rusty spade to cut the grass along the line of the cord, then doggedly removed the grass on the path side.

She dumped the sods in the wheelbarrow and pushed it along the stream to the back of the house, eventually forming a pile between a couple of shrubs. Afterwards she sat down on top of the mound of crushed slate. She panted, looking around. What could she use to line the path? The geese saw her sitting there and wandered over to the barbed-wire fence, gabbling loudly. She threw lumps of slate at them but they didn't seem to care. She didn't have enough strength left in her arm to make it that far.

In the pigsty she found two wooden posts, not nearly enough for the whole path. She descended the concrete steps to the cellar once again and sat down on the bottom step. The tiled floor was a pale green colour. Why was it so clean in here, so freshly swept? It was as if the room were used for something wet. She sniffed; there was nothing about the smell to give her a clue.

The Zuiderbad in autumn, the white changing booths beside the pool, the sandwich she ate on her way back home, the bare shrubs in a blanket of mist in the Rijksmuseum garden, the hum of the canal-side traffic. She thought of her parents in their upstairs flat in De Pijp, saw her mother making her swimming-pool sandwich, boiling potatoes, the window in the narrow kitchen wet with steam, everything lit brightly by the fluorescent light. They still lived there. With central heating now, smooth laminate floors, a new kitchen and a TV that was way too big for the tiny living room. And a message from their daughter. She had kept calling and hanging up until she got the answering machine – her father's voice, giving only his surname. 'I'm just letting you know I'm away. There's no need to worry. Really.' Thinking about it now, she wasn't happy with that *really*. It was completely unnecessary. Homesickness was something you could enjoy, but not always. Sometimes it made you weak, so weak that five concrete steps felt like fifty.

Alder branches. The three trees along the stream were alders. She knew because she recognised the small, round cones. It had been a long time since the trees had been pollarded. She knew the word, pollard, even though she'd never used a pruning saw to cut any kind of wood at all. Or did thick ivy stems count as wood? After lying on the divan for a couple of hours, she carried a kitchen chair outside. The chair Rhys Jones had sat on. She set it against one of the trees and climbed onto it in her muddy clogs. It's a shame I didn't do this early this morning, she thought. Then he would have had a mucky arse as well as holes in his socks. The saw did its work when she pulled – she felt that – not when she pushed. She also noticed that she had to think carefully about where to stand to make sure a branch didn't fall on her head. After sawing off five, she felt like she'd done more than enough work for one day and decided to stop. She cut the twigs and thin tops off with the new secateurs and dragged the branches over to the edge of the grass. By removing the sods, she had made a furrow along the path and now she laid the branches in that furrow, one after the other. She sat down on the step. It looked neat. The branches were thick enough to form a real border. Only now did she see that the grassy field was a lawn that someone must have mown relatively recently. The cows were gone. When she stood up, she discovered that they were quite far away. She hadn't noticed that at all, their walking away. A beautiful way of measuring the passing time: the sun that had suddenly leapt forward and was already quite low, a herd of cows that had silently and serenely relocated. She saw this for the first time and thought of her thesis.

21

Emily Dickinson. Despite her reputation (*probably the most loved and certainly the greatest of American poets*, according to the back of Habegger's biography), Dickinson wrote an awful lot of lazy rhyming quatrains, doggerel as far as she was concerned. She leafed through the *Collected Poems*, earth under her fingernails. It was night, pitch black outside but for the odd light in the distance. She drank a glass of wine and smoked a cigarette. Downstairs, a pan sat on the draining board with quite a bit of food left in it. The fire was burning. Never stung by a single bee, she mused. Bees everywhere: on a gentle breeze or in the clover. She thought of her university office: the cold computer containing all of her Dickinson notes and a very rough plan of her thesis, which was supposed to be about the plethora of lesser poems and Dickinson's all-too-eager canonisation; the pot plants; the steel filing cabinets; and, through the window, which looked out on a long, narrow street, snow. Habegger's indigestible biography – a doorstop full of question marks and nonsensical little theories (so exhaustive it even cites a coughing fit Dickinson's great-great-uncle suffered in the spring of 1837 as a possible explanation for a certain sensibility in her poetry) – had delayed her work for months.

She screwed up the piece of paper on which she had written 'curtains' (the window in the small bedroom was still uncovered) and picked up the soft pencil. She imagined herself outside in the daylight with her back to the front door, and sketched the lawn, the gently winding stream, the low stone wall forming an L around the grass, the pigsty diagonally opposite the house, the new, straight path along the front wall, the three alders and the three shrubs. Pity she didn't have any coloured pencils. There'd be a new path: from the front door straight through the grass, ending at the wall. There'd be flower beds. She tried to draw a rose arch, which proved much more difficult than she'd imagined. It ruined the sketch and she didn't have a rubber. She screwed up this piece of paper too. Sticking a new cigarette in her mouth instead, she picked up the *Collected Poems* and opened it at the contents page. She'd had this book for more than a decade – there were notes in it, the pages were stained, the dust jacket was torn – and now noticed for the first time how short the section titled LOVE was and how long the last, TIME AND ETERNITY. She started to cry.

22

The husband sat in the living room that was too small for the new TV. His wife's mother sat next to him on the couch, her father on a chair near the TV. Gusty November rain beat against the windows, a street light swung back and forth. The TV was on. It had been on the first time the husband came here, a good few years ago now, and every other occasion he had been here at night. Quite often during the day too, especially at weekends. They had turned the volume down five notches when he had arrived but it was still annoying. There was singing and judging, with blaring ads in between.

'It's almost December,' the mother said.

'Yes,' said the husband.

'This is really starting to upset me.'

'What can we do about it?' he asked.

'It's all your fault.'

'My fault?'

The mother gave him a look that said no further explanation was necessary and he should realise perfectly well that he was to blame.

'Yes,' said the father, without so much as a glance in his direction. Up till then he hadn't even opened his mouth.

'Yes, what?' asked the mother.

'Just, yes,' said the father.

She sighed. 'How can we start the festive season like this? St Nicholas. Christmas.' She gestured weakly at the windowsill, where three candles were already burning in a triangular holder. The flames were motionless; the windows were well insulated.

'Don't ask me,' said the husband.

'Bah!' said the father.

'What?' asked the mother.

'He can't sing at all!'

'Has she done this before?' the husband asked. 'I mean, before me.'

'Never! She never just disappeared. She didn't even like pyjama parties. She never stayed the night at friends'.'

'At my brother's, she did,' the father said.

'Yes. She never got enough of that. Staying at her uncle's. She never even mentioned her auntie. Those two were thick as thieves.'

'He taught her how to smoke,' said the father.

'Bah. That's right. And always putting ideas in her head. He used to say funny things to her. When she came home, it always took ages to get her back to her old self.'

'What kind of things?'

'That she had to be able to do things herself. That when it comes down to it, people are always alone. That you should never let other people tell you what to do.'

'That's not so bad, is it?'

'No, but she took it to heart, she upped and left. Her auntie was distraught, but her uncle just sniggered. And when she came home again, she wouldn't listen to us at all.'

'So she used to disappear.'

'No, an hour or so, never long. Two hours at most. When we heard about the smoking, that was it. We refused to let her stay there ever again.'

'My brother isn't . . . altogether right,' the father said.

'That's one way of putting it, I suppose,' the mother said. 'You could say he's mad as a hatter.'

'Come on . . .'

'I'm always scared that he' – pointing at her husband – 'is going that way too. Fortunately he's married to a very sensible, very strong woman.'

'Drink?' the father asked.

'Yes, please,' the husband said.

'Sure, hit the bottle. That'll solve things.'

'You too?' the father asked.

'No, of course not! Have I ever drunk a single drop of alcohol?'

'You're never too old to start.' The father got up and poured two old genevers: his own glass full to overflowing so that he had to bend over and take a slurp before he could pick it up. After putting the other glass down in front of the husband, he immediately returned his attention to the TV.

'Yes,' the mother said, sighing. 'Him going that way too . . .'

'*Ach*, woman.'

She started to cry softly.

The husband sipped his genever. He wondered if his mother-in-law was right, if it was his fault. A squall of rain briefly drowned out the singing of a fat girl with spiky hair who was standing motionless in a large room. She had a magnificent, clear voice and seemed to forget everything around her while she sang. Her eyes gleamed, her hands hung next to her thighs, completely relaxed, she became beautiful. Soon after, they told her that she lacked the 'necessary charisma'. Next, please.

'Bastards,' said the father.

During a commercial break, the mother started again. 'Are they going to put you in prison now?'

'No,' the husband said. In front of him was a second glass of genever.

'Why not?'

'Because I'm paying for all the damage.'

'So nowadays you can commit arson wherever you like without getting sent to prison?'

'That depends, I suppose,' the husband said. 'I didn't leave the scene. I cooperated. I think it's related to that.'

'Have you got the money?'

'Sure.'

'It's still your fault.'

'Why do you say that? Do you really think it's that simple?'

'Yes.'

'You *know* what she did.'

'Yes.'

'So how can it be my fault?'

'How do we even know it's true? We've only got it from you. Who says you're not lying?'

'Why would I lie?'

'Because of everything you've got to hide.'

'I don't have anything to hide.'

'No,' said the father, who was staring at the TV screen.

'You keep out of it,' said the mother. 'Where could that poor child have got to?'

'The uncle,' the husband said. 'That brother of yours. Is he still alive?'

'And kicking!' the father said. 'He's not even seventy yet.'

'Where's he live?'

'You think she's at his place?' the mother asked.

'She's not there,' the father said.

'He already phoned him. She's not there. Unless he's lying. That's quite possible too, of course. He's stark staring mad.'

There was more singing and judging on TV. The father had turned it up after his wife's last remark. He was sitting much too close; it was hard to believe he could see anything at all with his nose pressed against the screen like that. Or was it a way of making himself invisible, so that he could comment safely from the sidelines now and then?

'Money,' said the father.

'What?'

'Don't you get statements from the bank? Showing what's been withdrawn, where and when. She needs money, doesn't she?'

'I get statements,' the husband said. 'Not her. She does it all online. I don't have access. We have separate accounts.'

'If you ask me, you've got plenty to hide,' the mother said. 'You turned out to be an arsonist, after all.'

The husband sighed.

'Not having any kids, that's your fault too. I'm sure of it.'

'You're sure?'

'Yes.'

'Didn't she tell you about the tests?'

'What tests?'

'The tests I've had.'

'I don't know anything about that.'

'That's obvious.'

'I want a glass of wine.'

'What?' said the father.

'I said I want a glass of wine. White.'

'Help yourself.'

'You serve your son-in-law and I have to help myself?'

'Yes,' said the father. 'I'm watching TV. And you never drink.'

The mother stood up and walked to the kitchen. The husband pondered the ferocity she had put into the phrase 'son-in-law' and waited for his father-in-law to turn round. To say something to him. Man to man. Light flickered through the living room.

'Why do all these people make such fools of themselves?' said the father.

The husband shrugged.

'I don't get it.'

'Don't you want to be on TV?'

'Nope.'

'They do. No matter what.'

'In the old days she always used to look out the window on St Nicholas' Eve. She was the kind of kid who'd sit with her face up close to the glass and stare out at the wet streets.'

'What about the presents?' asked the husband.

'Yes, she was interested in them too, of course, but still . . .' The father looked at the screen. 'What bothers me most,' he said quietly, 'is that she said "really". There's *really* no need to worry.'

The mother came back. She was holding a glass that was quarter filled with wine. After sitting down and taking a mouthful, she pulled a wry face. 'So you're fine?'

'There's nothing wrong with me at all.'

'When was that?'

'Last autumn.'

'Did she get herself tested too?'

'No.'

'Why not?'

'Because she didn't think it was necessary?'

'Are you asking me?'

'No, I'm just saying.'

'If I were her, I'd get myself tested too.'

All three of them drank and stared at the TV. A youth in shorts and woolly socks with a bare, tattooed upper body leapt around the studio. He screamed all kinds of things, but they couldn't follow him at all. Maybe he came from the east of the country. The husband didn't want to think about the student. He wanted to stay calm.

'After all, it's getting pretty late in the day,' the mother said.

'*Ach.*'

'How old are you now?'

'Forty-three.'

'Were things going well with the two of you?'

The husband thought for a moment. 'No.' After a while he said it again. 'No.'

'He's a complete nutter,' the father said.

'What was the matter? What was going on?' the mother asked.

'*Ach.*'

'And now?'

'Wait a bit longer?'

'And then?'

'Maybe go to the police? I'll ask the policeman who questioned me what else we can do.'

'Do you still see him then?'

'After he took my statement, we went and had a beer together.'

'Why?'

'No reason. He's a nice guy.'

'Even though he should have thrown you in jail.'

'That wasn't necessary.'

'Police officers are ordinary citizens too,' the father said.

'What do you know about it?' the mother asked.

'*Ach,* woman.'

The husband couldn't help but notice how loving that sounded.

The mother took her last mouthful of wine. 'I still prefer a good cup of tea,' she said.

23

The bread was finished. She had dumped the cake in the bin; she'd gone off it. She decided not to drive to Waunfawr, she wanted to see if she was able to follow one of those dotted green lines, converting symbols on a two-dimensional map into real paths, hills, houses and fields. She pulled on her hiking boots, grabbed a rucksack and locked the front door. On the path in front of the house her heart sank. The cord she had strung was still there, the bamboo posts too. She'd have to move a lot of slate. She turned the corner of the house and walked down the drive past the goose field. Five were standing at the gate. She acted as if she hadn't seen them. The inquisitive faces, the quiet gaggling, the expectant shuffling. Five.

Map in hand, she walked through the oiled kissing gate. The green dotted line had told her not to follow her own drive, but the long grass hid every trace of a path. Shoulders hunched, she crossed the field at random and came out at a fence with a stile. She climbed over it and wanted to turn left. There was the neighbour's house; by the looks of things she'd have to walk right past it. A door seemed to be open. She hesitated and studied the map carefully before turning back, as if she were just a walker who had taken a wrong turning. Quickly she climbed up onto the stile and down again, crossed the field with the long grass and followed the drive to the narrow road. She picked up the green dotted line again a few hundred metres farther along, indicated in the real world by the sign with the hiker. When she stepped into the bakery after a walk that felt like it would never end, she saw that it was quarter to one.

'On foot?' the baker asked.

'Yes,' she answered, out of breath.

'No distance at all, huh?'

'No, here in no time.'

'We close at one. Just so you know next time. Awen!'

The baker's wife emerged from the back. 'Oh, hello, love,' she said. 'How was the cake?'

'Good. Rhys Jones was enthusiastic about it too.'

'Rhys Jones,' the baker said.

'He loves our cakes,' Awen said. 'Are you settling here permanently, love?'

'Where does he actually live?'

'Near the mountain. That way.' The baker gestured through the wall. 'In late October he moves his sheep to the old Evans farm.'

'Do you get enough customers here?' She was starting to feel hot and took a step to one side under the pretext of looking at something in the glass case under the counter.

'His wife died,' Awen continued. 'All very tragic, and if she was still alive she would never let him eat so much cake.'

'We get by.' The baker gave his wife a sideways glance. 'As long as people don't buy their bread at Tesco's . . .'

'Is there enough heating in that house?' Awen asked.

'It's fine,' she said.

'It's not too lonely and isolated for you?'

'No, that's not a problem. There are geese. And a lot of sheep now.'

'You're alone? No husband?'

'Mrs Evans came here to buy her bread right up to the end,' the baker said loudly, as if trying to drown out his wife.

'You should get a dog,' Awen said.

'What would you like?' the baker asked.

She wanted to ask what Mrs Evans had died of and how long ago, but the couple on the other side of the counter looked at her so expectantly and so inquisitively that she stuck to ordering two loaves of bread and two packets of biscuits.

'See you later,' she said, putting her purchases in her rucksack.

'When you run out of bread,' the baker said. 'And soon we'll have Christmas pudding.'

'A dog,' the baker's wife called after her. 'That's a true friend.'

She pulled the shop door shut and studied the sky. It was grey. Grey and drab, but it wasn't raining. She looked towards Mount Snowdon and remembered that she needed to keep the mountain on her left. She glanced back as she stepped off the pavement. The baker who didn't have a name and his wife Awen were standing there motionless, watching her. They didn't wave, they watched.

The route she took back wasn't exactly the same; almost everywhere she had gone wrong on the way there, she went right on the way back. Almost. But somewhere she made another mistake after all and it took her a long time to realise she had branched off on a different dotted line. It was all so indistinguishable: the thorny hedges, the squat oaks, the pastures, the metal drinking troughs, the manic birdsong. She found that strange: it was late November, why were the birds acting like it was spring? Without planning to, she came out at the T-junction where she had first seen the mountain and suddenly knew where she was; she didn't even need the map any more. She sat down with her back against a wooden gate, pulled a packet of biscuits out of her rucksack and ate half of them, giving herself plenty of time to study the mountain. Despite the grey weather it was covered with different colours: brown, ochre, green, even a shade of purple. It didn't look difficult, she thought.

When she carried on to the drive, it was as if it were already twilight. She had to bend over and grab a tree. When she stood up straight, the pain had nowhere to go; crouched over, the dull twinges seemed to spread out a little, becoming more bearable. She couldn't tell where precisely it was coming from: even in her arms and legs, it stabbed and nagged. She rubbed her belly and her upper arms, pressed a hand against her forehead and thought of her uncle. A little later, when she was picking her steps forward again, she saw Emily Dickinson before her, walking through her autumn garden, a first line in her head – *The murmuring of bees has ceased* – and trying to think how to help the poem along. No, never stung by a bee, our Emily.

24

The next morning she took her time over breakfast. She hadn't been eating well, regularly skipping her evening meal. She still drank plenty. The clock said half past nine. When everything in the house was quiet, she could hear it ticking:

sharp, spiteful little ticks. She didn't want it, she didn't want time in her kitchen. She wanted to stop the clock, but the thought of putting a chair under it was enough to make her feel sick with exhaustion. Stopping it, not just to get rid of time, but to thwart that oafish sheep farmer too. She thought about Rhys Jones a lot and it always wound her up.

She'd done her best to make something of the living room and the rooms upstairs; the kitchen was just as Mrs Evans had left it. There was a lingering smell of old woman around the sink and cupboards, an odour that, in the weeks she had lived here, she had gradually come to associate with herself. It even seemed to have impregnated the old-fashioned washing machine: immediately after she'd done a load, before she'd hung it out to dry on the rack at the top of the stairs, a musty air had already imposed itself on the fresh scent of washing powder. Yesterday at the baker's she had clearly picked up the smell of the old woman, perhaps because the walk had made her perspire, and she had stepped sideways to avoid her reflection in the narrow mirror behind the bread rack, scared as she was of seeing a different person.

She made coffee, whisked milk, cut two slices of bread and spread them with salted butter. She spread one with blackcurrant jam and put cheese on the other, then sat down and forced herself to eat and drink all of it. She looked out, saw that the creeper, silhouetted against the clear blue sky, was growing more and more transparent, and tucked a lock of hair behind her ear. She wondered if she should go to the hairdresser's for once. After washing the plate and mug, she went upstairs. Her diary was lying on the table in the study. She opened it and studied the dates, then worked forward from a date she was sure of and tore off a perforated corner. It was Friday 27 November.

She left the car in the deserted car park next to the castle and walked into town. In the street with the clock in the arch of the town wall – yet another clock – she found a hairdresser's. It was between the doctor's and the chemist's; she hadn't noticed it last time. If it hadn't been 27 November, if this had been a normal stay, she would have enjoyed this: walking straight to a hairdresser's in a foreign town as if nothing in the world could be more natural, as if she came here every month to have her hair done. Now the sun's reflection on the large window was too bright for her eyes, the bread was weighing on her stomach like concrete and she felt on the point of surrender, as if she were delivering herself up to a torturer with gentle hands. And she hadn't even gone in yet.

There was just one other customer, the doctor. He was sitting there smoking. A second cigarette was smouldering in the ashtray next to the mirror.

'Hello, love,' the hairdresser said. 'Sit yourself down. I'll just finish off this gentleman. I'm almost done.'

'Ah, the badger lady,' said the doctor. Everything above the cobalt-blue hairdressing cape looked like a newly hatched chick. He studied her in the mirror.

'What's that?' the hairdresser asked.

'The badger lady. A badger bit her on the foot.'

'No! That's impossible.'

'That's what I said, but it did.'

'How?'

'Lying down on a big rock with bare feet.'

'Really?'

'Yep.'

The hairdresser stopped working, standing with her comb hand and scissor hand poised in mid-air. 'I only ever see dead badgers. On the side of the road.' She reached out to the ashtray and sucked so hard on her cigarette that the tendons in her neck stood out. She used her other hand to wave away the smoke she exhaled.

'Me too. They're stupid animals. They think they own the night. That's why they never look out.'

'Is that it, do you think?'

'I don't know. I've lived here my whole life and I've never seen a live badger. Maybe you should ask the Dutchwoman.'

Now the doctor and the hairdresser both looked at her in the mirror. The small salon was thick with smoke. Fortunately she'd already picked a magazine up off the coffee table, stunned as she was at being discussed like this, and began leafing through it randomly. Nobody actually asked her anything, so she didn't need to answer. She tried to concentrate on an article about how to arrange pumpkins on a porch while the doctor went into detail about his patients' complaints. He had a strange way of addressing the hairdresser as an equal, as if they were two middle-aged women who had known each other for decades, two friends discussing everyday life. Cackling back at him every now and then, the hairdresser snipped away until the moment she whipped the cape off his shoulders and called out, 'Done!' The doctor got up out of the chair and thanked her. The hairdresser showed no sign of moving towards the till.

Standing in front of her, the doctor lit a cigarette. 'You coming by again?' he asked.

'Why?' she said.

'So I can check the wound. Among other things.'

'I don't think that's necessary.' She kept her eyes stubbornly fixed on a photo of an enormous green pumpkin.

'Whatever you think best,' the doctor said. 'Whatever you think best.' He left.

'Come and sit over here,' said the hairdresser. 'Then we'll start by giving your hair a nice wash.'

The hairdresser kneaded and stroked. Her hands were soft. The water was exactly the right temperature, the shampoo smelt very pleasant. As far as she was concerned, they could postpone the cutting for a while.

'How would you like it?' the hairdresser asked. 'A trim?'

'Short, please. Easy.'

'The badger. Was that really true?'

'Yes,' she said. 'And badgers come out in the daytime too.' They said nothing more during the wash. When it was finished, she thought she could smell Mrs Evans again, despite the shampoo. She looked at herself in the mirror – hair gone from around her neck, face pale, eyes dark – and knew that she was going to ask for something she had never asked for before. 'Could you perhaps turn me round?'

'What?'

'Turn me round. The chair.'

'But why?'

'Because I . . .' She didn't know how to explain it.

'You won't be able to see what I'm doing.'

'I'm confident you'll do a good job. I like surprises.'

'This is a new one on me,' the hairdresser said, turning the chair with her foot. 'I can't see what I'm doing properly now either.' She tapped a cigarette out of the packet and set the door ajar, after first opening it all the way and looking left and right down the street. Then she laid the burning cigarette on the ashtray. 'Is this a Dutch custom?' she asked.

'No.'

'Well, here we go then.' A quarter of an hour later she was finished. No new customers had come in. The hairdresser used a dryer to dry the gel she had rubbed into her hair and pulled it into shape with rough tugs. The cigarette had burnt down unsmoked.

She got up without turning to face the mirror and walked over to the small counter with the till on it.

'Don't you want to look?'

'No. I really do want it to be a surprise.'

The hairdresser stared at her and opened her mouth, perhaps to ask if that was another Dutch custom.

'I like surprises,' she said.

Deeply insulted, the hairdresser closed her mouth and typed an amount on the old-fashioned cash register, which rang loudly.

She paid, said a friendly goodbye and walked out of the salon, leaving the door slightly ajar. A little way down the street she glanced back and saw the hairdresser standing outside her shop, one arm crossed under her breasts with the hand tucked in her armpit, a cigarette in the other hand, staring fixedly at the perfumery across the road, her bleached hair thin in the slowly rising cloud of sunlit cigarette smoke.

She kept a grip on herself through the narrow streets and the car park, even though there was hardly anyone around. It was only when she was sitting in the car and saw herself looking like a startled animal in the rear-view mirror that she began to cry.

25

She inspected the wood supply in the pigsty, looking and counting, and decided not to light fires in more than one room at a time. Then there'd be enough. And if she did run out, she could always sit in the kitchen near the cooker.

The sun was shining again and the smoke from her cigarette rose straight up, just like the hairdresser's yesterday. She leant against the light-coloured wall of the sty and felt its warmth on her back through her nightie, but her neck was cold to touch. Her head was light, as if kilos of hair had been cut off. She smoked with her eyes shut.

Here she was, without a single appointment, without a single obligation. She thought of the geese and the cord strung along the path and remembered one commitment she had made – to buy bread from the baker in Waunfawr – then felt like everything was too much. She threw the cigarette onto the lawn and went into the house, wiping her bare feet off on the mat to get rid of the slate grit. She dressed, put a towel in the rucksack and went for a walk.

*

On her own path. Across the stream and through the oiled kissing gates and the small wood of ancient trees, where the path grew clearer each time she used it. Song from birds she couldn't identify and had never known; a squirrel. She walked straight through the stone circle and onto the embankment through the marshy ground. The map was back home on the kitchen table. Past the boggy section, she came to a steel gate with long-haired, big-horned black cattle on the other side. A stile next to the gate. She'd have to cross the field. She didn't hesitate, but climbed over, paying no attention to the cattle. If I pretend they don't exist, they won't notice me either, she thought. The path seemed to follow a wooded bank. If necessary, she could crawl into the thick undergrowth for safety. The countryside kept undulating and when she looked back after fifty steps, she didn't recognise a thing. She was lucky: the frame of what had once been a kissing gate showed that she had taken the right direction. She left the black cattle behind her. In front of her the land sloped down; she could see the water.

The trees here were almost completely leafless, the grass yellow and grazed close to the ground, here and there a clump of thistles. On the bank was an upright stone, the kind they called standing stones on the map, but this one looked like the work of a farmer with heavy machinery. Walking around the large pond, she saw concrete banks and a small brick building; inside, she could hear water flowing but couldn't see where it came out. That confirmed her idea that the pond was man-made, some kind of reservoir. An asphalt road came to a dead end behind the building. The water before her was so smooth and motionless it made her think of a freshly polished silver tray. It was clear and viscous, but didn't look cold. She undressed next to a big rock she could lay her clothes on, then broke the water by dipping the foot with the scar into it. It was cold, but not cold enough to put her off. The bottom felt rock hard under a thin layer of mud, like an enormous concrete slab that had been cleaned fairly recently. Walking as slowly as possible, she waded out to the middle where – with the water up to her waist – she stayed until the last ripple had died away and it was smooth again. She could see her toes and her knees, minuscule air bubbles on each pubic hair, a strange refraction of the light at her belly and forearms, as if the lower body belonged to someone else and didn't fit properly. She looked around and, yes, this bank too had neither a beginning nor an end. Like a circle. Maybe she didn't feel cold because, without the slightest breath of wind, even the weak sun was able to warm her upper body, and because she continued to think of the water as viscous, slow and heavy. She remained standing there and understood perfectly why her uncle had been so indecisive in that hotel pond: the place itself had robbed him of the ability to decide. It was only when she saw goosebumps appearing around her nipples that she waded back to the bank. She had seen time passing in the rotation of the long shadows of the trees, the arrival of a school of tiny fish at her toes and their departure, and the appearance of five sheep next to the standing stone. Was this it, what Emily Dickinson had done for almost her entire adult life? Had she tried to hold back time, making it bearable and less lonely too perhaps, by capturing it in hundreds of poems? And not just TIME but also LOVE and LIFE and even NATURE. It doesn't matter, she thought. It's not important any more, and anyway, those sections weren't even Dickinson's idea. She dried herself and put her clothes back on, walking away from the water long before the last ripples had died down.

The black cattle were gone, or at least no longer visible from the path along the wooded bank. On the embankment, it occurred to her that this path must have been well used at some stage, otherwise they wouldn't have put up the signs with the hiker or added kissing gates and stiles. No matter how natural she found its current state of abandonment, walkers must pass by occasionally. Maybe they already had: when she was getting her hair done or shopping at Tesco's or lying on the divan. She smoked a cigarette on the largest rock in the stone circle and sat waiting until the badger – she always assumed it was the same one, the 'male' that had bitten her foot – appeared under the gorse. As before, it looked at her without giving any sign of wanting to leave its hiding place. Maybe it remembered the branch breaking on its back.

26

After docking at Hull she had visited four different cashpoints with both her credit card and her normal bank card and withdrawn a large amount of money. She was still nauseous – the night boat had pitched and rolled and she had felt so miserable she had resolved never again to travel on such a huge ship – but clear-headed enough to realise that transactions could be traced and know that was something she didn't want. She started driving, sticking to main roads. Bradford, Manchester, Chester. She was thinking of Ireland. At a Little Chef she had to pull the tarpaulin tighter over the stuff she had in the trailer. 'Stuff', that was how she thought of it. The single mattress, the coffee table, things she'd bundled together. Even before she reached Wales, Holyhead appeared on the signs, straight ahead on the A55. She filled up the car and paid with her credit card before she realised what she was doing. In Bangor it finally stopped raining and when she drove onto the Britannia Bridge for Anglesey, she remembered the crossing. No, not another nightmare like that. The strait between the mainland and Anglesey looked magnificent in the damp sun: the steep wooded shores, the two old bridges, big white birds in briny mud, a small island with a white cottage. She turned back and went looking for a bed and breakfast. The next day she ended up at the estate agent's run by Rhys Jones's 'friend', who said he had the perfect house for her, almost fully furnished and available to rent quarterly. A greystone Welsh farmhouse. They went to have a look in his car. He gave her a tour, pointing out the shed with a throwaway gesture and saying 'pigsty'. After a second night in the B&B, she moved in. He hadn't mentioned the geese and she hadn't noticed them. Rhys Jones's sheep arrived later. She paid until 31 December and still had more than enough money.

She was wheeling half-loads of slate from the mound to the path very calmly. Every time she rounded the corner of the house with the empty wheelbarrow, the five geese cackled quietly. She could hardly bear it and started shovelling faster and faster to cover the sound. After a few loads she was only quarter filling the wheelbarrow. She had removed the cord and the bamboo posts and tipped the grit between the thick alder branches, using the rusty pitchfork to spread it. When she was finished, she slid a kitchen chair up to the cooker, drank a glass of milk, ate a sandwich, smoked a cigarette and thought that, if she really wanted to feel like a gardener, she should start smoking roll-ups. In the afternoon she used a knife to dig weeds out of the slate grit while kneeling on the doormat. She slid slowly from the corner near the pigsty to the corner with the bamboo and the oil tank and carried on all the way to the stream, where she laid the doormat – which said WELCOME – down as a cushion. While working, she didn't think consciously, all kinds of things just flitted through her mind. Now she sat with her legs dangling down the steep bank and stared at the fast-flowing stream, which fell quickly here. Growing on the steep bank opposite, little more than a metre away, were various kinds of ferns and many other plants she didn't know by name. At some point a tree had fallen and come to rest across the stream like a mossy bridge. She found it difficult to tear herself away from the water; its rushing and bubbling were hypnotic, never-ending. Did this stream rise on the mountain?

That night she stared at the fire just as she had stared at the water. She had lit candles and put them on the window-sill. Nagging pain in her back. Before getting into the bath, she had eaten some bread with cheese and a sweet onion. Hot meals were too much trouble. Fruit and vegetables were healthy but, of course, things like that only applied to people who were healthy. She'd always found meat difficult. What, for Christ's sake, was she going to do with the lamb Rhys Jones had threatened her with? She had thought about it while lying in the hot water, and about the garden. Despite failing to produce a sketch, she had already laid out paths in her imagination: the flower beds were in bloom and she had even built the rose arch. Now she stared at the fire without really seeing it. She had warmth, she had light. With cushions, the divan was a fine place to lie down. She hadn't dressed again after her bath and had a soft blanket draped over her. A glass of wine on the coffee table next to *The Wind in the Willows* and the unread books.

There was a sweet and spicy quality to the smell of the burning wood that made her think of the home-made *borstplaat* and *speculaas* her grandmother used to make and bring to their flat in the Rustenburgerstraat; her grandparents themselves; the pounding on the door when St Nicholas left a sack of presents; looking out through the misted window at the street – preferably in bad weather – and always amazed to see people walking there, with any luck catching a glimpse of a Black Peter on a bicycle; knowing that it was cold and wet outside and warm inside; chocolate milk and presents; the rustle and special smell of the wrapping paper; the laughter of grown-ups in a dimly lit living room; checking her own wish list, sometimes with a pencil to cross off the presents she'd received; knowing that it would all be over the moment the fluorescent light in the kitchen flickered and turned on; the thumping on the stairs once she was in bed; the empty feeling of 6 December. That homesickness kept coming back. Maybe there was another word for it, maybe nostalgia was better. It had more to do with a time than a place.

The geese started to honk loudly. I need a stereo, she thought, struggling to her feet. She hurried downstairs, flicked on the outside light and ran down the path next to the house. 'Hey!' she shouted. 'Fuck off!' She grabbed a handful of crushed slate and threw it in the direction of the goose field, which was engulfed in darkness. 'Go away! Go away!' Another handful of slate. 'Hey!' A single stone rolled out of her hand, but the stream drowned the sound of its falling. The geese were quiet. She sank to her knees and looked up at the sky. Never before had she seen so many stars. Never before had she looked up at them naked on her knees in late November.

December

27

Tidying up the garage, the husband dropped a cardboard box on his foot. The box contained books and papers belonging to his wife. *Academic year 2003–2004* was written on the side. He was trying to push it up onto a high shelf when a piece of tape came loose and he lost his grip. The box hit him on the chest and landed corner-first on his left foot. He was wearing flip-flops. He made it through the day – it was Sunday 6 December – by going easy on his foot and calling off the tidy-up, spending the whole afternoon in front of the TV with a glass of red wine: sport and more bloody sport. The next morning his foot was swollen blue and yellow, so swollen the smallest toes were no longer recognisable as separate digits. After looking up the number in his address book, he phoned their GP. They were able to fit him in straight away, but he had to look up the address on the Internet first. He pulled on running shoes without doing up the laces and tried to avoid changing gear as much as possible; depressing the clutch was torture. He wouldn't be training any time soon. It was no problem to keep the car in third as the route from home to the practice was all within his own neighbourhood. On the way he called work, playing it safe by telling them he was worried it might take all day. He found it hard to believe it wasn't broken.

*

He didn't recognise the doctor when he went in, a woman, when he'd been almost certain his doctor was a man. She shook his hand firmly, told him her name and sat down, half hidden by a computer screen.

'Fertility test,' she said. 'Requested November last year.'

'Um, yes,' he said.

'Carried out at the VU hospital.'

'Is this an exam?' he asked.

'Sorry?'

'What are you doing?'

'I'm familiarising myself with your history.'

'A box landed on my foot. A very heavy box.'

'Yes, of course.'

'Sorry?'

'I mean . . .'

'Who are you, anyway?'

'I just told you my name.'

'Yes, I heard you, but my doctor has a different name.'

'Since 1 January this has been a group practice. That means that several –'

'I know what a group practice is.'

'Your foot, you said.'

'Yes.' He pulled off his shoe and sock.

'Could you come over here and sit on the bed, please?'

While the doctor examined his foot, and none too gently, he tried to read the computer screen over her head. The bed was too far from the desk. I must be less irritable, he thought. Minutes later he was sitting opposite her again. She wrote a referral.

'Back to the VU?' she asked.

'Yes,' he said. 'That's easiest.'

'I think it's just severe bruising, but I don't have X-ray eyes.'

'No,' he said.

She handed him the letter. 'You can go straight there.'

'That information,' he said.

'Yes?'

'Is that just mine or is it ours . . . together?'

The doctor peered at the screen. 'Everyone living at your address. For instance, it says here that your wife – or girlfriend – also had a fertility test.'

'Yes, of course,' he said.

She stared at the screen and either typed something or used the arrow keys; he couldn't see. 'July.' She read something, then met his gaze directly. 'How is she now? In the middle of treatment?'

'It's going OK,' he said.

'It's not often that something else shows up during a fertility test. They're not looking for that kind of thing.'

'No,' he said. Keep talking, he thought. Please, keep talking.

She was still staring straight at him. 'You don't have the slightest idea what I'm talking about, do you?'

'No. Yes.'

'I'm sorry, I can't say anything else. I'm afraid I've said too much already.'

'She's my wife!' he said.

'Yes. That's what makes it so peculiar. Your not knowing.'

28

Mist. The world stood still. There was hardly any noise, even the stream sounded as if the water was being sieved through gauze. She was working in the garden all the same. The first alder was now cut back completely and she had already lopped a couple of thick branches off the second. She set about it very calmly. When she felt that she was tiring, she carefully climbed down off the kitchen chair and went inside to sit for a while in front of the cooker. It was only after drinking a cup of tea, having a snack and smoking a cigarette that she went out again. She stripped the side twigs off the branches and stacked them against the garden wall on the short side of the lawn. In weather like this, Dickinson would have sat inside coughing and sighing, she thought, writing about bright spring days and the first bee. The sawing was easier now she'd learnt to let the saw do the work. The light was on in the pigsty, the door open; it looked warm in there. The diffuse glow in the mist made her think of donkeys and oxen standing round a crib. Keep sawing like that, she thought. Very calmly, in a small world, all sound muffled. Working outside, she imagined the kitchen table with the map on it and a new attempt at a garden design, which made her think of Monday and driving to Caernarfon, where she could buy coloured pencils. And another shop where she planned to buy a TV: the nights really were getting very long now and she wanted to be able to empty her mind watching a gardening or an antiques programme, or that BBC series about people who want to move from the city to the country and call in the presenters' help.

As she was carrying the umpteenth branch over to the garden wall, someone vaulted it in a swirl of wet air. It was like the jump happened in slow motion, perhaps because of the large rucksack the man was carrying. He landed on the pile of branches, lost his balance and slid sideways. That too seemed slower than normal, reminding her of a gymnast doing a floor exercise. He struggled to right himself, clutching his left wrist. She stopped where she was.

'Oh,' he said. It wasn't a man, more a boy.

'Have you hurt yourself?' she asked.

'No, not really,' he said. 'At least . . .'

She dropped the branch and walked up to him.

'Bradwen,' he said.

'What?'

'That's my name.' He held out a hand.

She put her hand in his and said, 'Emilie,' pronouncing it the Dutch way.

'Is this your garden?'

'Yes.'

'Are you German?'

'What is it with you people? Can't anyone here tell the difference between Dutch and German?'

'Sorry.' He rolled his Rs.

'It doesn't matter. But it is peculiar.' She was still holding his hand. He was wearing a woolly hat and he squinted.

Only slightly, but enough to be confusing. 'Have you hurt your wrist?'

'Yes.'

She removed her hand. 'Would you like to sit down for a minute?'

'Yes, please.'

'Come inside then. I'll make some coffee.'

'Sam!' the boy shouted.

A dog jumped over the low wall. Like its master it landed on the branches, and like its master's, its feet slid out from under it. It scrambled back up.

'A dog,' she said.

'Sam,' the boy said. 'That's my mate.'

'Hello, Sam,' she said.

The dog sniffed her outstretched hand and licked it.

'He likes you,' the boy said.

She gripped the animal under its chin and looked into its eyes. 'I like him too.' The dog pulled his head free.

'Nice,' said the boy.

'Coffee,' she said.

The boy had put his rucksack under the clock and taken off his hat, revealing thick black hair. He didn't run his fingers through it. The dog lay on the floor against the cooker and let out the occasional, contented sigh. She had made some coffee and lit a couple of candles on the windowsill above the sink. The sun was already low. She had cut some bread and made a cheese sandwich for the boy. 'Thank you, Emily,' he said when she put the plate down on the table in front of him, pronouncing it the English way. What difference does it make?

she thought. He'll be gone again soon. Now he'd finished the sandwich and drunk a second cup of coffee. He hadn't spoken while eating and drinking. He'd taken his hiking boots off at the front door; there was a sweet smell in the kitchen.

'I'd better be off,' he said. 'It's getting dark.'

'Where are you going?'

'There's a bed and breakfast a bit further along.'

'How much further?'

He reached over to his rucksack and pulled out a map. The very same map she'd taken off the table earlier, folded and laid on the worktop, though his had been used a lot more. The stiff paper had already turned soft. He unfolded it and ran his index finger over it. He had sinewy hands with broad thumbs, a little dirty.

'Two or three miles.'

'It will be pitch black by that time,' she said.

'Yes,' he said.

'Do they know you're coming?'

'No, I haven't rung yet.' He thought about it. 'Usually I ring up around twelve, after I've walked a couple of hours. Not today. I don't know why.'

'If necessary, you can sleep here,' she said. 'If you'd like to. There's a divan in the study.'

The dog yawned.

'Sam thinks it's a good idea,' he said. 'He's nice and warm there.'

'It's settled then.'

'Do you live here alone?'

'Yes.'

*

The boy had a bath while she cooked a meal. The dog had slipped away from his warm spot in front of the cooker and when she quietly climbed the first half of the staircase she saw him lying in front of the closed bathroom door. He raised his head and watched her attentively. She shook her head and went downstairs again and the dog followed her. Strange, how easily the boy and the dog adjusted to this house. She put a few more logs in the stove in the living room. She stirred the soup. The dog lay down with its back against the cooker. She opened a bottle of red wine. The clock ticked sharply, the geese clucked softly.

29

'I'm mapping a new long-distance path,' he said. 'Planning it, actually. In the south they've got the Pembrokeshire Coast path. Now they want a path up here too.' He had taken a notebook out of his rucksack. 'I write everything down, all the things I see, landmarks. Sometimes a whole day's work is wasted because I come to a dead end.' He had washed his hair and looked very different from earlier. As if there were a glow around his head.

'How long will it take you?'

'I don't know. I've got all the time in the world.'

'Why is that?'

'I dropped out of uni. I couldn't be bothered any more.'

'How long have you been at it so far?'

'A week and a half.'

He had tipped dry food from a plastic bag into a bowl for Sam, who finished it in no time. There was a pan of soup on the table. Bread, beetroot salad, cheese and butter.

'I have to talk to farmers too. Ask permission. Farmers and homeowners. So I'm actually working as we speak.'

'The path follows my drive for almost half a mile.'

'Exactly.'

She poured him another glass of wine. He'd gulped down the first two and now he started to tip this one back as well. 'Are you scared someone else will drink it?' she asked.

'You pour it, I'll drink it.'

'How old are you?'

'Twenty.'

'What were you studying?'

'I've forgotten. It was boring.'

'You don't want to say.'

He rushed through his soup. Instead of bringing the spoon up to his mouth, he brought his head down to the bowl. 'Nice.'

'How's your wrist?'

'No problem.'

'Would you like some more?'

'No, I've had enough, thanks.' He leant back, raised both arms and stretched by pulling one wrist with the other hand. His faded T-shirt crept up, there was a hole in the left armpit. 'Not that you can say no anyway,' he said.

'What?'

'You can't actually refuse. Right of way. That's what it's called. The path I took today already exists. It's on the map. You can't stop people using it.'

'I've never seen any walkers here at all. I'm the only one who uses that path.'

'Yeah, it was funny today. At a certain point the path suddenly appeared and was easy to follow, but before that I kept losing my way.'

'I walk on it to the stone circle.'

'The stone circle?'

'Yes, you walked right through it.'

'Didn't notice a thing.'

'It was misty.'

'I wouldn't mind another glass of wine.'

She had to stand up to fetch another bottle. The dog was immediately alert. It was warm in the kitchen, the window had misted over. She smelt the old-woman smell again and shook her head to get rid of it. The boy and the dog had their own smells, especially the dog, and she hadn't put the lid back on the soup pan. A pan which, by the way, had belonged to Mrs Evans. She opened the bottle. 'Where do you come from?'

'I was born in Llanberis. You?'

'Rotterdam.'

'Never been there.'

'I haven't been to Llanberis either.' She tried to make her LL sound just like his.

After they'd drunk the second bottle, she'd had enough. She was exhausted, she needed some paracetamol and she wanted a bath. While he'd been sitting at the table freshly washed and wearing clean clothes, she'd been in her gardening clothes. She had deliberately called him Bradwen a few times to get used to the name and, as if in response, he'd kept calling her Emily. Or was it the other way round? Had she started calling him by name because he kept ending sentences with hers? She had a constant feeling he was about to say something important, even after he'd started on his concluding 'Emily', perhaps because he kept looking at her with that squint, behind which she also suspected more than if he'd looked at her normally.

'I'll light the fire in your room. Then I'll have a bath and go to bed.'

'Fine,' he said.

'There are books there. Mostly English.'

'I've got my own book with me. Can Sam sleep there too?'

'That's fine by me. I'll lay a rug on the floor for him.'

The dog was already heading through to the living room.

'I'll let him out first.'

'See you in the morning.'

'Goodnight,' he said. He put on his coat and followed the dog, closing the front door behind him. Sam barked angrily a couple of times.

She went upstairs and laid a fire in the grate, looked around to see if there was anything she should put away, and fetched a duvet cover from her bedroom. 'Yes,' she said to Dickinson's portrait after making up a bed on the divan. 'Yes, this is a different kettle of fish. See you later.' Then she went into the bathroom and pushed two paracetamol out of a strip. In a fortnight or so she'd almost finished all five boxes. Taking a painkiller was the first thing she did in the morning. She avoided looking at herself in the mirror, which wasn't difficult with it steamed over from running the bath. A little later she was lying in the warm water, her mind a blank. She heard the boy and the dog come upstairs. He pulled the door to the study shut behind him. The dog barked and stopped almost immediately when the boy warned him to be quiet. 'Not again,' she said quietly to her toes. 'And definitely not now, Emilie from Rotterdam.' She rubbed her belly with both hands, keeping it up for several minutes, then ran her fingers, almost surprised, through her hair, which was very short.

30

The next morning she got up fairly early. The door to the study was closed and the house was silent. She made some coffee and set the table, putting a tablecloth on it for the first time. The mist had cleared in the night, a dull sun was shining. The sight of the one and a half unpollarded alders immediately drained her. He would leave; she would have to do it alone. She sat down with her hands next to her empty plate. Instead of coming down from upstairs, he came in from outside, bringing the bitter smell of fallen leaves into the house with him. The dog was overjoyed to see her. She could still see the boy as a gymnast: not a brawny one on the rings, but the slender kind whose best event is the floor exercise. He took off his coat and hung it on the back of the chair he was about to sit down on, opposite her.

'Good morning,' he said.

'Good morning,' she said.

'I was at the stone circle. It's a real one. This bit will definitely go in the route.'

'Are some of them unreal then?'

'Sure. Even farmers have time on their hands sometimes.'

'See any badgers?'

'No. You only see them at night. Sam didn't smell anything either.'

She pulled off a sock and stuck her foot out towards him under the table.

'What's that?'

'A scar.'

'Yes, I can see that. What from?' He reached out to her foot and for the first time since the bite she felt the teeth penetrating her flesh. Just before he was about to touch her skin, he pulled back his hand.

'A badger. In the daytime.'

'That's impossible.'

'Are you calling me a liar?'

He stared at her with his strange, slightly evasive eyes. Last night it had been worse. His squint. Probably because of the wine. 'No,' he said.

Her thigh muscle started to quiver so she put her foot down on the floor, then pulled the sock back on. She poured the coffee. 'Did you sleep well?'

'Yes. With the sound of the stream.' He started to eat. The dog sat next to his chair and kept its eyes on him, head slightly crooked. 'You'll get yours, Sam.'

She buttered a slice of bread, put some cheese on it and looked at it. She swallowed. 'Heading off soon?'

'Yes.'

A bit of coffee then, she could always manage that. The boy ate in silence, the dog following every piece into his mouth. Bradwen looked in turn at his plate, out the window and at the dog. He glanced once at the clock. 'I want to go to Snowdon today,' he said. 'Have you got a suggestion?'

'A suggestion?'

'The most beautiful way to get there.'

'Can you walk it in one day?'

'Easy. I'm not going up, just to the foot of the mountain.'

'I haven't gone in that direction yet.'

'How long you been living here?'

'A month or two.'

'Is it temporary?'

'No. Permanent.'

'Wow.' He'd finished eating and rubbed his hands which, despite last night's bath, were still a little dirty. 'Your turn, Sam.' He tipped some dog food into the bowl in front of the cooker. 'I'll get my stuff from upstairs and then I'll be off.'

'OK,' she said.

Ten minutes later they were standing at the corner of the house. The grass was wet, the door of the pigsty open. The alder branches lay gleaming against the garden wall. The boy shook her hand. 'Thank you very much,' he said. The dog followed the barbed-wire fence, sniffing and barking. The geese were in the far corner of the field.

'You're welcome.' She waited before letting go of his hand.

It wouldn't be strange to say something else now, but she didn't know what. He'd put on his woolly hat, though it wasn't cold. 'I'd better get Sam away from those geese.'

'You go straight ahead at that bend. I oiled the kissing gate a while ago.'

He carefully pulled back his hand. 'See you,' he said. He walked off, whistling the dog, which was now running back and forth along the fence. She could only see his legs, an elbow now and then. Man and dog: man with restless legs, kicking a chunk of slate along in front of him. Just before he went through the kissing gate, Sam ran up to him. There was no squeak, she'd oiled the hinges well. He was gone. The dog barked one last time.

She walked over to the goose field. The birds came up to her. Four. It must have happened the night she'd knelt there naked, gazing up at the stars. A whole week had passed without her giving the geese a second glance. She ran into the house, grabbed the chunk of bread off the worktop, ran back, pulled off little pieces of bread and threw them over the barbed-wire fence. She looked at the shelter she'd made. The chicken wire that was supposed to cover the entrance was still folded back. Maybe they crept in at night and weren't safe even then. Now that she was standing with bread in her hands and had the geese's attention, she remembered the day she'd tried to herd the birds into the shelter. Lying wet and exhausted on her side in the grass, she had thought of luring them with bread. The next day Rhys Jones showed up and it was his fault she'd forgotten about the geese. How could I have let that happen? she asked herself. Neglecting animals

I'm responsible for because I think someone's a bastard? Where's he got to anyway? It's already December and November is the month for slaughtering animals. What's keeping him? She moved along to the gate and went into the goose field. The birds followed her. She scattered some bread in front of the shelter. They weren't having it. As if knowing she was trying to trick them, they kept a good distance. She sighed and went back to the gate. After she had tied it up again with the piece of rope, the geese ran to the shelter and started gulping down the bread. '*Godverdomme*,' she said quietly. 'Pig-headed, stupid creatures.' She looked at the kissing gate and the gap in the row of oaks. Slowly, she walked back to the house. In the kitchen the breakfast things were still on the table. She picked up his plate and smelt it, then put his mug to her lips. The house had never been this empty. She didn't think twice, but grabbed her bag and ran to the car.

31

Music filled the house; a large radio-CD player was set up on the kitchen sideboard. The TV was just inside the front door in its box. She'd do that later. There were felt tips and coloured pencils on the table. She did the washing-up, humming along to the songs she knew and thinking, *See you*, not *goodbye*. See you, not goodbye. It could have been a line from a Dickinson poem, although hers mostly alternated between six and eight syllables. The short distance she had run earlier that morning felt like a marathon. She lowered the milk pan into the suds and stared out through the window. The study. She hadn't been in the study yet. She quickly dried her hands and went upstairs. She could tell how he'd got up from the way the duvet was lying on the divan: he'd thrown it off in one go and hadn't straightened it afterwards. I need to rest, she thought. I'm tired. She took off her clothes and lay down on the divan. It was cold in the study, the fire had burnt out long ago. The duvet cover chafed her nipples. The sweetness and the smell of bitter leaves she had noticed earlier came together at the top edge of the fabric. She pulled the duvet over her head and ran her hands over her belly.

Later, after she had put her clothes back on and lit a fire, she searched the room. Had the pile of books on the coffee table been disturbed? Had he written on the sheets of blank paper on the table next to the open volume of Dickinson's poetry? She couldn't remember if she had left it open at this page. A COUNTRY BURIAL. If, she thought, if this was where he had stopped leafing and reading, then . . .

She sat down and stared out of the window because she didn't know what came after 'then'. The sea was visible again over the tops of the now almost leafless trees. But far, very far away. She remembered something, also vague and far away, and stood up to rummage through a cardboard box of books she hadn't yet unpacked. She had been almost certain that Habegger's biography was in her office in Amsterdam, but it turned out to be in the box after all. She sat down at the desk and riffled the pages. On page 249 – where the book fell open – there was a thick red line under 'since nothing is as real as "thought and passion", our essential human truth is expressed by our fantasies, not our acts'. It was a reference to a book Dickinson had read when she was twenty-one which was supposed to have formed her, along with her great-great-uncle's coughing fit and all kinds of other insignificant events. Habegger was an old gasbag, but she still copied the passage onto the open page of the poetry volume, a little fearfully and with an empty feeling in her stomach, before closing the biography. Not just emptiness, but pain too, a bit higher than usual today, inhabiting her throat and the back of her head. She walked to the bathroom and took two paracetamol. It was almost time for her to see the doctor. She couldn't go on like this much longer. She wondered if she was up to it. Until yesterday she had been almost certain she was.

32

That afternoon she pushed the bamboo stakes down into the lawn. She had found a wooden slat in the pigsty, sturdy and more or less two metres long, and was using it as a measuring stick: three lengths into the lawn and one length wide. She turned it into a rectangle by stringing cord between the stakes. Slowly she started to cut a line in the grass. She wasn't thinking about removing the sods yet, but worked out that it was twelve square metres. Now and then she straightened her back, raising her head to the sun. Suddenly a dog stuck its head between her legs.

'He missed you too much.'

She turned round. The boy was standing next to the pigsty, one shoulder against the wall. The dog appeared unsurprised by their return. He sniffed around the oil tank, then disappeared behind the house.

'And now he's seen you, he's off again.' He didn't move from his spot. 'Not me though.'

'What happened?'

'Nothing. I couldn't arrange a place to sleep. Everything's shut around here this time of year.'

'Did you walk all the way to the mountain?'

'No. If I had, I wouldn't be back by now.' He held up a paper bag. 'I've brought something to eat.'

'From the baker's in Waunfawr?'

'Yes. They'd shut the second time I passed by, but she was still cleaning up. She said to say hello.'

'How did she know you were coming here?'

'They asked. They asked where I was coming from and where I was going.'

'And you told them?'

'Of course. Why not? She gave Sam a treat too. "A dog for the Dutchwoman," she said. "That's good."'

The dog started barking, probably at the geese.

'Sam ran ahead the whole way. As if he knew exactly where we were going.'

'Can you draw?'

'Yeah. Depends what.'

'A garden?'

'Oh, a plan. Sure. Why not? If I've got enough paper.'

'Can you connect a TV?'

'I'd say so.' He looked at the roof of the house. 'There's the aerial. You must be able to plug it in somewhere inside.'

'Can you dig, and push a wheelbarrow?'

'Of course.'

'Cook a lamb?'

'Definitely. With garlic and anchovies.'

'You can stay another day.'

He nodded and finally came free of the pigsty wall.

'Anchovies?'

'Then you don't need to add salt.'

'You haven't had any coffee since this morning, I suppose?'

'No. If they ever turn this into a long-distance path, the guidebook will have to say it's less suited for the winter months. Or not at all.' He gestured at the pigsty. 'You could turn it into a bed and breakfast.'

'Come on,' she said.

'Sam!' he called.

The light brown cows had come up to the garden wall without her noticing, but took off in all directions when the dog came running round the corner of the house. The sun was almost setting; her working day was over.

33

The husband moved his foot. The plaster was heavy and awkward; a chair wobbled. The bar was half full. Lots of couples with their heads close together, the men with beers in front of them, the women mostly with glasses of Coke. A plastic Christmas tree in one corner, pine branches and fairy lights over the bar.

'How'd you do it?' the policeman asked.

'Box of books.'

They drank their beers.

'I found out something that made me want to track her down after all.'

'What?'

'*Ach.*' The husband raised his glass to his lips.

'The police can't help you,' the policeman said. 'She left of her own free will. There aren't any signs of coercion.'

'What should I do then?'

'Hire a private investigator.'

'A private eye? Do they really exist?'

'Do you have any idea how often people use services like that?'

'Apparently not.'

'Look on the Web sometime.'

'Can you recommend one?'

'Nope. And if I could, I wouldn't be allowed to.'

'Is it expensive?'

'Quite. But they often get quick results.'

The husband pointed at the policeman's empty glass.

'I'll get them. You can hardly walk.' The policeman stood up and went over to the bar for two more beers. He said something to the barman, they laughed, then he slalomed back to the table.

'Are you married?' the husband asked.

'No. I'm in a relationship though. With another officer.'

'Have you ever . . . Do you ever have someone else?'

'Of course. That's dead normal for us.' The policeman looked him straight in the eye. 'Why do you ask?'

'Just curious. Man talk, you know.'

'That's a disappointment. So you had girlfriends?'

'*A* girlfriend. Just one. But she did it too.'

'What's the big deal? You lot always make it so difficult.'

'Yeah, maybe. Women are different from men.'

'No, they're not. How?'

'When they're unfaithful, there has to be an underlying problem.'

'So your wife had an underlying problem?'

'Yes.'

'You want something to eat with this?'

'Sure.'

'I'll get some *bitterballen*.'

'What are we doing here?'

'What do you mean?'

'Why do you associate with me?'

'Aart! One portion of *bitterballen*!' the policeman called. The barman nodded. More and more people came into the bar, bringing in the damp. The windows misted over.

The husband drained his glass.

'Why do *you* associate with *me*? I could ask you the same,' the policeman said.

'I thought you were a nice guy.'

'I am. Have you tried to get hold of that student?'

'No. I don't have any contacts at the university. What's the point? I'd guess he's not attending lectures any more.'

'He'd be out of there.'

'Travelling maybe. Somewhere in Asia. India, probably. To find himself and find enlightenment.'

'Oh, one of them. Ending up on a mattress on the floor of some filthy hovel with all his Imodium gone. And a kid screaming day and night in the room next door.'

'Yes. Maybe. Thanks.'

'You're welcome.'

'My mother-in-law thinks it's strange me going out for a beer with you. She thinks you should have put me in jail. Is the barman one too?'

'Yep.'

'Hmm.'

'Aart! Two more beers!'

'There's a side of her I've never understood. A part that was always out of reach. It's like, it doesn't really surprise me, her being gone.'

'What did you find out? To make you suddenly want to register her as missing?'

'She's ill.'

'Ill?'

'Maybe very, very ill.'

'And now she's gone away, like a cat crawling off?'

'Yes, maybe. She's gone away anyway. From me. And from her parents.'

The barman put two glasses of beer down on the table. 'The *bitterballen* are coming,' he said, laying a hand on the policeman's shoulder for a second.

'That's awful.'

'At the end of the last academic year she started

something with this student.' He looked around. 'Maybe because she was ill.'

'The one whose dick you wanted to cut off.'

'Oh yeah, sorry. You already knew that. We were just talking about him.'

'I said it wasn't allowed.'

The husband looked at the policeman. 'It's only now that I realise it must have been funny. For you.'

'It wasn't the least bit funny.'

'No, of course not. But I was angry.'

'Even though you weren't much better yourself?'

'No. I'm not angry any more. And I want to understand why she did it.'

A woman put a plate of *bitterballen* down between them. 'Careful,' she said. 'Hot.'

'Thanks,' the policeman said.

'It's not even what she did,' the husband said. 'But her having done it. Someone doing things, secret things, things from which you – me in this case – are completely excluded.'

They both ate a *bitterball*.

'Go online when you get home,' the policeman said. 'Find one and give them a call.'

'Yes.'

'You really have no idea where she's gone?'

'No. Abroad, I think.'

'Why do you think that?'

'How long can you stay in hiding here?'

'For all we know she could be round the corner. The closer you are, the further away.'

'That's true.'

'So your mother-in-law wanted you in jail.'

'Yeah. She thinks it's all my fault.'

'And your father-in-law?'

'He says "no", "yes" and "*ach*, woman". He takes it all in his stride.'

They ate the rest of the *bitterballen* in silence, washing the heat off their tongues with beer.

'Shall we take in a disco?' the policeman asked.

'Jesus, man.'

'How much longer?'

The husband looked down at the cast on his foot. 'Three weeks or so. It was her books.'

The policeman laughed.

The bar grew busier, noisier. The barman gestured at the policeman in a way the husband didn't understand. He stood up, grabbing his crutches. 'I'm off before it's too crowded for me to get through.'

'Keep me up to date.'

'I will.'

They shook hands. The husband paid the tab on the way out and when he turned back at the door, he saw the policeman sitting at the bar. The barman watched him go. It was raining. He hobbled to the tram stop, trying to imagine what a real-life private investigator would be like. In the glass hoarding there was a poster of a skater in a vest, advertising bread. A taxi sped by in the tram lane, splashing water up over the plaster cast.

34

'Rotterdam,' Bradwen said. 'Is that a nice city?'

'Well,' she said. 'Not really. It's ugly actually.'

'Is that why you're here now?'

His hair was tousled, he'd come straight from the divan, and never before had she so longed to run her fingers through it. She had already noticed the particular way he had of sighing, and when he did, it was almost impossible to resist touching him on the head. The dog seemed to have picked up his sigh. It was only natural for him to ask questions; people talk to each other. Maybe she needed to pre-empt him. '*Ach*,' she said, pouring the coffee.

'I think that's a beautiful word,' he said.

'*Ach*?'

'Yes. We don't have a word like that. One that means "Shut up, you".'

'Eat,' she said.

He cut the bread, tossing a crooked slice to Sam, who had found a fixed spot in front of the cooker. He smeared on a thick layer of butter. The traffic news was on the radio. While he ate, he drew circles on a piece of paper, alternating between yellow and brown felt tips. 'What are we going to do today?' he asked.

'The garden.'

'And the TV?'

'Oh, yes. Do that first.'

'Fine.' He passed her a slice of bread. 'You're not eating.'

'I've never eaten much in the mornings,' she said.

'OK.' He stood up. 'I'll go and brush my teeth.' The dog went upstairs with him.

She got up and went over to the kitchen window. It was misty again and still. Good weather for working, but she had to lean on the draining board. She lit the two candles on the windowsill and hummed along with the radio. The cooker warmed her. Water ran in the pipes. He turned off the upstairs tap, sending a loud clunk through the whole system. The boy and the dog came back down. She heard him open the front door. 'Go and catch some grey squirrels,' he said. Before he came back into the kitchen, she wiped her cheeks with the back of her hand.

'Grey squirrels?' she asked.

'Immigrants. Taking the place over.'

'Just like me.'

'Yes, you're an immigrant too.'

'But you don't set the dog on me.'

'Of course not.' He gave off a sharp smell of toothpaste. 'Living room?'

'I think so.'

He walked out of the kitchen. Rhys Jones in socks had been laughable, but that didn't apply to Bradwen. His were hiking socks, blue and grey, the kind with an L and an R. She heard him pace through the living room, where she kept the standard lamp on all day. Distant barking came from outside, from the far side of the stream by the sound of it. 'Got it!' the boy called.

She went into the living room. He was standing in a corner holding a cable that came down through the ceiling.

'Now there's a moment's tension while we see if we can plug it in somewhere on the TV,' he said.

She needed to sit down. The boy in the yellow light of the lamp, happy to have found the aerial cable; the wood-burning stove whose coals she had raked over like Cinderella earlier that morning, blowing to get it burning again without matches. She watched him lift the TV out of the cardboard box and put it on the floor in the corner. He went down on one knee and fiddled with the back of the set, his T-shirt creeping up to reveal a strip of lower back above the waist-band of his jeans. 'Done it,' he said. 'Now, a power point.'

'There.' She pointed to the double socket the lamp was plugged into.

He plugged the TV in too and turned it on. A picture appeared immediately: a rough sea, people in rowing boats bobbing around what looked like the wing of a small plane. '*Real Rescues*,' Bradwen said. 'Every morning from quarter past nine to ten o'clock.'

'Fantastic,' she said. 'Turn it off.'

He turned it off and stood up. 'Shall I carry on with the trees?'

'If you don't mind. I find it very heavy work.'

'Of course I don't mind.' He looked at her.

'Are you going to finish that path too?' she asked.

'Sure. It's my job. That's what I get paid for.'

'But not tomorrow?'

'If that's OK by you. My time's my own.'

'Mine too,' she said.

'Maybe we can do a section together?'

'I would very much like to go up that mountain sometime.'

He went upstairs and came down soon afterwards with his coat and hat on. 'Do I use a kitchen chair?'

'Yes. It's still out there. I forgot to bring it in.' She didn't move from the sofa, even though she wished she was standing next to him at the front door.

He pulled on his boots and went out, calling the dog. A gust of cold air blew into the room. She lit a cigarette.

After a while she got up to put a log in the stove. Then she swept the kitchen floor. An old kettle was steaming gently on the cooker. Now and then she looked out. Sometimes Bradwen was standing on the chair sawing, sometimes he carried a branch to the pile against the low garden wall and disappeared almost entirely in the mist. The dog was nowhere in sight. She wondered if he'd noticed that she'd lain on his divan.

35

She sat on the sofa in the living room watching *Escape to the Country*. Bradwen was doing the shopping in the car. Sam was lying at her feet. While an agitated couple walked around on the screen with the woman shouting, 'I'd rather die than give up my cats,' she wept silently. The wood-burning stove, the big cooker, the new TV and radio, the boy and the dog, the garden. 'Dog,' she said and Sam raised his head, licking the back of her hand. How on earth had Dickinson done that, withdrawing further and further, writing poetry as if her life depended on it, and dying? The life of the spirit, human truth – or authenticity? – expressed through the imagination and not by deeds. She sipped her red wine. Always red wine, as if it were some kind of tonic. Her uncle used to drink a medicinal glass of Pleegzuster Bloedwijn every night. Did they still make that? Red wine fortified with health-giving minerals? 'Watch the cat,' said the woman on TV. She climbed a staircase with a hideous carpet, neither stroking nor paying any other attention to the cat, which was lying on one of the steps. At least, she assumed her uncle drank a glass every night; she didn't know what he did when she wasn't there. She wondered what the boy would bring home. She had wanted to give him a shopping list but he wouldn't have it. He also refused the money she tried to give him. She thought briefly about her husband and saw him before her: pulling the laces of his running shoes tight, straightening his back and opening the door. Gone. Would he be sitting at home now, quietly drinking a beer and thinking, She'll come back? She took another mouthful of wine and lit a cigarette. Here, she thought. I'm here. Now. The Englishwoman was standing in a garden with a view of a meadow. 'I can imagine myself living here. Dogs in the garden and a horse in the shed over there.' Fucking cow, she thought.

Sam lifted his head from his paws and looked at the door. The next thing she heard the car, then the door slamming, footsteps on the crushed slate. I don't understand, she thought. How I was able to bear it here alone for weeks on end?

'You in here smoking again?' Bradwen nudged the dog out of the way with his knee.

'Yes,' she answered. The sight of the open door made her shiver.

'It's bad for you.'

'I know.'

'Fish,' he said. 'I bought fish and I'm going to cook up a storm.'

Fish, she thought. I'll have to switch to white.

Bradwen was stirring something in a saucepan on the cooker. Sam had been fed and had called it a day; he was snoring softly on the rug in front of the stove in the living room. She looked at the boy's back while absent-mindedly drawing circles on the piece of paper he had drawn circles on earlier. With a blue felt tip. She had already set the table. 'What's your surname?' she asked.

'Jones.'

'Is everybody here called Jones?'

'Yep. What's yours?'

'I'm not telling,' she said.

He turned round, smiling.

'What difference does it make?' she asked.

'None.' He went back to his calm stirring. She got up and walked round the table to stand next to him. He looked up, stuck an index finger in the sauce and held it out to her, and without thinking she licked it. She nodded. He nodded too and continued stirring. It was as if he had been cooking here for weeks. She took the box of matches from the window-sill and lit the two candles. She fetched a candlestick from the sideboard, put it on the table and lit that too. When she sat down again she heard the sharp ticking of the clock.

'A man called Rhys Jones came here one day,' she said.

'Uh-huh.'

'The sheep in the field by the road are his.'

'Are you renting this house?'

'Yes. He had all kinds of arrangements with the former resident. He scoffed almost half a cake and he had holes in his socks.'

The boy looked at her blankly.

'I detest him. He's coming back with a lamb.'

'I'm here now,' he said.

Yes, she thought. You're here now.

Bradwen put the saucepans on the table and pulled a dish out of the oven. 'Haddock.'

She had no idea what kind of fish that was and didn't care. It smelt good and she would do her best to eat as much as she possibly could. Lured by the smell, Sam came and sat next to *her*, not his master. 'Why do dogs do that?' she asked.

'He knows I won't give him any. You're a kind of alpha female now.'

'An alpha female?'

'Dogs think we're dogs too.'

'I'm a person,' she told the dog. 'A female person.'

Sam tilted his head to one side, doing his best to look sad.

Bradwen dished up: potatoes, broccoli, fish and sauce. He poured wine too. White wine. He raised his glass. 'To Rhys Jones,' he said.

'Why?'

'He's going to bring us a lamb. It's December.'

A cramp twisted her belly, she couldn't look him in the eye. She stabbed at the fish and took a bite. It was as soft as butter. She chewed and swallowed. She took another bite.

'Is it good?' he asked.

'Delicious,' she said, bowing her head.

'What is it?'

'*Ach.*'

She heard him stand up. Out of the corner of her eye she saw him push the dog aside with one knee. She felt a hand, a whole forearm on her back and smelt his breath. She pressed her head against his stomach. 'I'm glad you're here,' she said. She looked down past his trouser legs at the neatly swept kitchen floor. A sock with an L and a sock with an R. Broad feet.

'I'm here,' he said.

'Why are you here?' she asked.

'*Ach,*' he said, or tried to say. His Welsh CH wasn't the same as her Dutch CH.

She straightened her neck and reached over her shoulder to take his hand. 'Eat,' she said. 'It will get cold.'

Bradwen padded around her and back to his chair, setting her hand down next to her plate on the way. Sam turned from one to the other with a slightly wild look. The boy sat, picked up his wine glass and raised it. 'December,' he said.

She smiled. 'December.' She ate everything on her plate and drank another glass of wine to go with it. Now that he was pouring, he didn't drink so greedily.

'I'm going to start on Emily Dickinson tonight,' he said, drawing out his pronunciation of her first name.

It didn't matter. It was all right if he saw through her. Maybe he wasn't called Jones either. Maybe a time would come when she would ask him, would want to ask him. I don't think I want to know anything about him at all, she thought. He just has to be here.

36

Two days later the sun was shining. After standing with her back against the pigsty, feeling how the pale bricks had soaked up the warmth, she said, 'Come.' The smoke from her cigarette rose straight up into the air. Mist hung between the trunks of the trees along the stream. The boy lowered the wheelbarrow full of crushed slate. He had already removed the grass from the rectangle in the lawn and lined it with alder branches.

'Coffee?' he asked. He had pulled his hat up so it was perched on the back of his head, sweat gleaming on his forehead.

'No, we're going for a walk.'

He looked around. 'Sam!'

'He can't come. We have to lock him in the house.'

'I'll put him in the shed. He'd tear the place apart. He can't stand being alone.' The dog came running up past the oil tank. Bradwen grabbed him by the collar and dragged him into the pigsty. 'Let's go, quick.'

They followed the garden wall to the kissing gate.

'Why don't we just climb over the wall?'

'I can't.'

'You're not *that* old.'

'No, I'm not that old. Do you have any idea how old?'

'I don't care.'

They went through the kissing gate and followed the garden wall to the beams over the stream. The light brown cows were grazing at the other end of the field, a good bit lower down. They could hear howling from the pigsty. Bradwen stayed behind her, even where the path was wide enough to walk side by side. There was a car driving somewhere; she couldn't work out where the sound was coming from, which reminded her of the steam train and made her imagine the boy sitting next to her on a wooden bench in the train. She climbed the stile, expecting at any moment to feel a hand on her hand or a knee against her calf. At the stone circle she caught a smell of coconut again. She wondered if it was the gorse flowers. She sat down on the largest stone and gestured for the boy to come and sit next to her. He did. 'This is where I was lying,' she said, 'when the badger bit me.'

He sniffed a little and slid back and forth.

'You don't believe me, do you?'

'No.'

'Sit still.'

She pulled a packet of cigarettes out of her coat pocket and lit one.

'What are we doing?' he asked.

'Don't talk.'

*

After smoking a second cigarette she gave up. 'Let's go,' she said.

'What didn't happen?' he asked.

'Every time I sit here, a badger sticks its head out from under those bushes.'

'In the daytime?'

'Yes, of course. Or do you think I come and sit here in the middle of the night?'

'I've never seen a badger. Not a live one.'

'I have. I've seen it three times.'

'Uh-huh,' said the boy.

'Come.'

At the stile, things went fuzzy. Then everything turned dark purple and when she came to her senses again she was leaning on a crosspiece, the boy pressed up against her back with his arms wrapped around her. She saw thick grass, a rusty barbed-wire fence, tree trunks and rotting posts, mud. She heard Sam whimpering, realised vaguely that he was probably howling very loudly a long way away, and she heard agitated chirping. What kind of bird is that? she thought. I want to know. No time, no time. She smelt something sour, a smell she had until recently taken for the smell of fallen leaves or wood, the plank her hands were resting on. She felt the boy's body, which felt stuck to hers along the entire length of her trunk. He was breathing on the back of her neck, his forearms clamped around her belly as if he were scared something would fall out of her. 'There, there,' he said, encouraging her to stay calm. Like her '*ach*' had been for him, it was a kind of English without a Dutch equivalent. She didn't know if he'd realised that she'd already come to. I have to eat, she thought. I have to eat more. Something moved in a tree, sliding down a trunk. A grey squirrel ran across the path. It stopped, sitting up straight with its tiny front paws crossed discreetly across its chest. It seemed to look at her, then scampered off. Would a little creature like that think that I'm a slightly oversized squirrel with a second squirrel on my back? Does a squirrel see people the way a dog does? She didn't straighten up, she wanted the boy to hold her like this a little longer. She watched the squirrel until it ran up a tree just down the path. It all happened without a sound. The bird had fallen silent. I have to send him away, she realised suddenly. He has to leave. I can't have this. 'I'm not going to fall over,' she said.

The boy let go of her. 'A minute ago, you fell over.'

'Not any more.'

'Can you climb over it?'

'I think so.' She lifted a foot and put it on the lowest rail. My badger foot, she thought. She put the other foot next to it. She saw that she was going to manage and moved a hand from the plank to the post. Standing on the other side, panting slightly and turned to face the boy, she saw the black cattle she had seen the day she went to the pond. They were as black as his hair and her gaze sank from his hair to his eyes. Dark grey. She couldn't look straight into his eyes, she could never look straight into both his eyes, she always had to choose left or right.

37

Bradwen was cooking again. He did it without asking and seemed to enjoy it. Tonight he'd made spaghetti with a sauce that, whatever else it included, had a tremendous amount of garlic in it. 'It's healthy,' he said. 'You should eat as much garlic as possible.' In the afternoon the wind had started to pick up and it was still rising. There had been a gale warning on the radio. A branch from the creeper beat against the kitchen window. 'That branch has to come off the Chinese wisteria,' he said. She tried to feel positive. There was someone here who made decisions, who told her what needed doing, who – when necessary – held her tight. Without waiting to eat first, he asked where the secateurs were and went outside with a kitchen chair. She could just make out his legs, lit by the two candles on the windowsill. The dog had stayed inside, but was standing in front of the cooker with his ears pricked and his head up. Chinese wisteria, she thought, but what's it called in Dutch? She could hear the wind whistling in the living-room chimney, the wood-burning stove roared. A bottle of red wine was open on the kitchen table.

'You have to go,' she said when he came back in.

His hair had all been blown in one direction. He was holding a wisteria branch.

'To the next bed and breakfast. And then to another one, a day's walk from there.'

'No way,' he said. 'I am now going to dish up your dinner and then I'm going to pour you a glass of wine.'

'Tomorrow,' she said.

'No.'

'Dish up, then. And pour.'

Bradwen laid the branch on the floor and poured two glasses of wine. During dinner he smiled. He didn't say anything but kept smiling, drinking wine, refilling their glasses and finally running his fingers through his hair. He quietly whistled the dog, rubbed an eye with one finger and licked his knife.

'You don't take me seriously, do you?' she said.

'No.'

She sighed and tried again to feel positive, which was significantly easier after one and a half glasses of wine.

'I'm staying,' he said.

'We'll see.'

'The garden's nowhere near done and I assume you want to have it finished by a certain date?'

'What makes you assume that?'

'It's just a feeling.'

'I have feelings too sometimes.'

'Really?'

'And I find them rather tiring. Just pour some more wine instead.'

The wind was now howling around the house. Despite being cut back, the bamboo was scraping the kitchen wall. Now and then something blew against the window. The dog was asleep but restless, whimpering and with his legs twitching.

Bradwen topped her up. 'He's dreaming,' he said.

'So what did you think of Dickinson?' she asked.

'Nothing.'

'Nothing?'

'I haven't read it. I don't get poetry.'

'Another reason you should go.'

He smiled again, or rather, he continued smiling. 'Coffee?'

'Have you got a mobile?' she asked.

'Yes.'

'Do you ever use it? I haven't even seen it.'

'No. I don't know anyone.'

'That's nonsense, of course.'

As if the dog had understood, he woke and barked once. He stood up and went over to stand panting where the kitchen joined the living room.

'I'd be careful if I were you,' the boy said. 'He bites.'

'Do you have a father and a mother?'

He hesitated. 'Of course.'

'You know them, then. Don't you need to call home sometimes to tell them how you're doing?'

'I'm here now.'

She had a tremendous desire to grab her breasts to try to make something clear. She almost did it, but instead – her hands checked in mid-air – she knocked her glass over and began to cry. The boy didn't do anything, he just stayed where he was. She stood up and walked to the stairs, passing the dog, who licked the back of her hand. She ran the bath, squeezing a long squirt of bubble bath into it, Native Herbs. She left the door – which was the only one inside the house you could lock – unlocked. She took off her clothes and stepped into the water. In the end, this was where she felt best: lying back in hot water, aware of her body, which felt flawless and uncompromised, especially with the storm raging outside. She saw the corridors of Dickson's Garden Centre before her, rows of rose bushes, and thought of bees in late spring. Come on then, she thought.

38

The windowpane clinked. Just when she thought the last gust had been the strongest, the wind roared even louder. She plunged deeper under the duvet, her bedroom door swung ajar, clatter from the landing. She held on tight to her body, hugging her breasts through the thin fabric of her nightie, putting her hands between her legs, raising her knees as if to brace herself, giving off a smell of bottled herbs. The wind roared in from the Irish Sea. She shook her head to dislodge an image of a big ship, pints of beer and fried snacks sliding over a bar, paintings hanging away from the wall, roulette balls bouncing across a red carpet, a clown on a small stage, off to one side, vomiting into the wings. She swallowed and imagined Bradwen on a blue-edged square, moving exclusively in diagonals. Wearing shorts but with his L and R socks on. They'd slipped down a little. He turned circles on his hands, elbows tucked in, the veins in his neck swollen. Sam was sitting on a chair on the edge of the blue square and barked as his master tumbled through the air, almost flying, and landed straight-legged in the dead centre of a corner before raising one outstretched arm, exposing his armpit. Above the raging of the storm something creaked. It was more tearing than creaking: old, living wood coming free of the earth. She realised that she was no longer thinking about before, her mind was clear of all memories of the husband, the student, her uncle, Christmas with the sweetly perfumed Santa-shaped candles. 'Ah,' she said, because that candle was in her head now, burnt down to Santa's waist, a puddle of red wax on the paper Christmas tablecloth, next to a plate of cauliflower cheese and thinly sliced roast beef. Along with her mother, who could never enjoy Christmas dinner because she was too scared to take her eyes off the candles in the Christmas decoration on top of the TV. She considered getting up. Going downstairs to sit next to the cooker and smoke? Maybe make some tea?

She shot bolt upright, threw the duvet aside and stood up. She held a hand against the window. She could feel the pressure on it. Things went black for a second; she'd got up too fast. The lights in the distance flickered. No, it was the branches swishing back and forth and blocking out the light as the storm rose and fell. She pulled the door further open and groped her way to the stairs, one hand heavy on the rail of the landing. Downstairs in the living room the stove was still smouldering, a vague red light lit the WELCOME mat at the front door and the boy's hiking boots, next to the mat.

She lit the two candles on the windowsill and put the kettle on the hottest plate. The bamboo scraped over the side wall and somewhere a door banged, the door to the pigsty, she could hear the metallic clang of the old-fashioned handle. It wasn't raining, the window was dry. The water started to boil. She filled a mug and dropped in a tea bag. While the tea brewed, she massaged her forehead and temples, her belly. Nothing. On the outside, there was nothing. She took the packet of cigarettes from the table and lit one. The tea was hot. She burnt her tongue and swore under her breath. Immediately after stubbing out the cigarette, she lit another. She sat on a chair between the table and the cooker and turned her head towards the clock. The wind was making such a racket she couldn't hear the sharp ticking. It was ten past two. She heard another kind of ticking. It was coming from the living room and when the dog appeared in the kitchen she realised it had been his nails on the wooden stairs. 'Hey,' she said. The dog hung his head and approached slowly, contrite, though she couldn't imagine what he had to be contrite about. 'Couldn't you sleep either?' she asked. Sam looked at her attentively, followed the smoke coming out of her mouth, then laid his head on her knees. His sigh made the bottom hem of her nightie tremble. She stubbed out her cigarette and laid a hand on his head. 'Where's your master?' she whispered. The dog started to whimper softly.

39

The next morning there was no wind at all. Bradwen stood next to a fallen oak that was lying with its crown over the stream. He pulled on a branch, holding the saw ready in his other hand. He had already rehung the pigsty door, which had blown off its hinges. She watched him with her belly pressed against the cooker. She held the mug she had drunk tea from hours before under the tap and watered the three flowering plants on the windowsill. Sam ran across the lawn with a branch in his mouth. The cows stood at the garden wall and watched, inquisitive and skittish. She brushed some crumbs off the worktop with a flat hand and sniffed. Was it the kitchen that smelt of old woman or was it her? The coffee pot started bubbling gently.

'I think it's going to snow,' the boy said when he came in. 'It's got cold.'

'Uh-huh,' she said without turning.

'Then we'll go to the mountain.'

'Don't you have to continue with your path?'

It was quiet behind her for a second. 'Sure.'

'But not now?'

'Not now.'

She sighed.

'I've got other things to worry about now.'

'Such as?'

'Rose beds. A Christmas tree.'

She turned round without moving away from the cooker. 'A Christmas tree?'

'Yep. It's almost Christmas.' He stood next to the table with his hat in his hand. His black hair was stuck to his forehead, there were oak chips on the collar of his coat. Today the L and R socks were red and blue.

'Do I need to wash some clothes for you?'

'You don't need to,' he said. 'But I do have dirty clothes.'

'All right, you dig and I'll wash.'

He looked at her but didn't speak.

'And now I suppose you'd like some coffee.'

'Yes, please.' Finally he sat down.

'Where's the dog?'

'Running up and down along the fence of the goose field. He's been doing it a while.'

'Why?'

'No idea.'

'Do you know anything about geese?'

'Not really.'

She poured a coffee and put it on the table in front of him. 'Biscuit?'

'Yes, please. Aren't you having one?'

'No.'

'Why not?'

'Bradwen,' she said. 'Stop it.'

'OK,' he said. 'But you haven't said "*ach*" yet.'

She smiled and laid a biscuit next to the coffee mug. Then she walked past him to the sideboard and turned on the radio.

'Yes,' said the boy, just loud enough. 'That's another method.'

She was standing at the front door to ask him what he wanted washed, but the sight of his bent back restrained her. He was digging, she went to do the washing, hauling herself up the stairs with her left hand on the banister. She went into the bathroom first to take a paracetamol, then crossed the landing. It had been a few days since she'd even been in the study. It was cold, the window above the oak table was up a little. The *Collected Poems* lay as she'd left it, the note she'd written was a little shaky. She rested three fingers on the page and looked down into the garden. The boy was working systematically: he'd already dug up a large part of the bordered rectangle, furrow by furrow. Now he'd stuck the spade in the ground and was standing at the open door of the old pigsty, looking down into the cellar. There was steam rising from his shoulders, his coat was lying on the garden wall. What did he see there? *Be its mattress straight.* Since Bradwen had come, she'd hardly given Dickinson a thought. She went over to the mantelpiece, where a brown rectangle with four metal clips was leaning against the wall. Apparently there was something about the portrait the boy didn't like. She turned it round.

From the mantelpiece, she walked to the divan to straighten the duvet. Behind the divan was a pile of clothes: jeans, L and R socks, a T-shirt, a couple of pairs of underpants. His rucksack was in the corner. She hesitated, then quickly bundled up the clothes. Before leaving the room she looked out through the small back window. The dog was still running back and forth near the geese, nose to the ground, the birds themselves huddled together near the shelter. The sky was a yellowish grey.

In the kitchen she squatted down next to the washing machine and put his clothes in one garment at a time. Whether it hung in the kitchen or seeped from the washing machine or anywhere else, the old-woman smell didn't stand a chance against the rancid pong of his blue and grey socks. He has to go, she thought. Better today than tomorrow. To fill the machine, she stripped the bed in her room and added the duvet cover, sheet and pillowcase to the load. *Be its pillow round.* On the radio Wham! were singing 'Last Christmas'.

40

This time the red-headed boy at Dickson's Garden Centre had a very different look on his face. He was wandering the car park in a red Santa hat, helping where help was needed. When he saw Bradwen, who had come out of the exit just behind her carrying a Christmas tree, he stopped in his tracks. She saw him wavering: he could hardly pretend he'd been approaching someone else. It was snowing lightly. All of the garden-centre employees were wearing red Santa hats and there were decorated Christmas trees everywhere, even between the tables in the Coffee Corner. A Christmas carol was playing on the PA system. The roses had been moved to make room for racks full of candles and other Christmas paraphernalia; it took her a while to find them. After picking out twelve rose bushes, she asked Bradwen to choose a Christmas tree, but only because she thought they could plonk it in the corner, decorate it and be done. He took one with roots. That was handy, he said, because you could plant it in the garden in January. When she saw him dragging the tree through the aisles, she realised she'd need baubles and tinsel and fairy lights.

The pots with the rose bushes rattled on the big trolley; she could barely look at them. Her head was aching.

'All right?' the redhead asked when she walked past him. 'Yes, I've got help today,' she said, giving him a sideways glance. She heard Bradwen say, 'Hi, mate,' in a rather jovial tone of voice, which undoubtedly meant something. The boy looked away, scanning the car park. Sam, who was sitting in the car, began to bark excitedly.

Bradwen drove very carefully up the drive; the snow was an inch deep. She sat with her hands on her lap and counted the geese. All four were still there and now, because of the whiteness around them, she saw how filthy they were, how bright the orange of their beaks. The sheep were much blacker than usual. It was only when she looked ahead at the house that she saw the tyre tracks.

'Someone's been here,' she said.

This time there was no note on the door.

How long since I gave those animals something to eat? she thought. Later, taking the geese a few chunks of bread, she saw that the tyre tracks ran over the field and that the sheep were crowded together near the fence.

41

In the morning the snow was two inches deep. The leaves of the rose bushes, which the boy had put down next to the freshly turned soil, were white.

'I have to go to Caernarfon,' she said after breakfast.

As usual, Bradwen had eaten a lot. The coffee was just ready.

'What are we doing there?'

'Me.'

'What are you doing there?'

'None of your business.'

'Do I need to drive?' He tried not to look hurt.

'No.'

He didn't say anything else.

'Thank you,' she said.

'What do I do?'

'Please yourself. Maybe you should call your parents for once.'

He sniffed and gestured over one shoulder with a thumb at the staircase on the other side of the wall. 'Thanks for washing my clothes.'

She lit a cigarette. 'Light the stove in the living room and make a fire in your bedroom too if you like.'

'There's not much wood left.'

'When it's gone, it's gone.'

'Shall I decorate the Christmas tree?'

'If you like.'

'Where?'

She glanced around the kitchen. There was an empty corner next to the sideboard. She gestured with the cigarette. 'There?'

'That's a good spot. Then we'll see it from the living room too. What shall I put it in?'

She didn't look at him. She couldn't look at him. What do you put a Christmas tree with roots in? She stubbed out the cigarette. 'There might be something in the pigsty or out the back. I don't know.'

'I'll find something,' the boy said.

The dog scrambled to its feet, walked over to her and began to lick her hand. She started to cry.

The boy didn't get up. 'There's no need to cry,' he said. 'I don't know why you're crying, and if I asked, you'd only say *"ach"* and that wouldn't get us anywhere. But there's no need to cry.'

'No,' she said, sniffing.

'When you get back from Caernarfon, from whatever it is you have to do there, the Christmas tree will be done and the stove will be lit in the living room. I'm going to Waunfawr in a bit, so there'll be fresh bread too. Not that you're bothered about eating, but it will be here. And I'm not going to ring my parents. I'm not going to ring anyone, because I'm here now. This afternoon at quarter past five, you'll sit on the sofa and turn the telly on and watch *Escape to the Country*, and while you're doing that, I'll cook. Fish. You'll eat it and drink two or three glasses of wine to go with it and maybe after tea we'll plan a garden together or watch a film. The BBC always show great films around Christmas. Afterwards you'll go to bed. If you like, I'll light a fire in your bedroom an hour beforehand. I can take the car and trailer and go for new wood any time I like. I can even pay for it. Sam and I will be sleeping two doors along. We're here. We're waiting for the lamb that farmer, Rhys Jones, promised you.'

She sat down. 'Yes,' she said. 'The lamb. He was here yesterday.'

'I saw.'

'He brought hay for the sheep.'

'I saw that too.'

'I keep thinking you're a gymnast.'

'What?'

'The kind that does floor exercises.'

'That's a first.'

'When you walk, when you sit, when you're sawing or digging.' She went to light another cigarette, but didn't, because then she would have had to smoke it and all she wanted to do was have a bath. To have a bath, then leave. She stood up. 'You say "we" a lot,' she said.

'That's because we're here together.'

'I think that's what made me cry.'

'Liar.'

'Yes.' She left the kitchen. In the bathroom she pressed the last three paracetamol out of the strip and took them with a couple of mouthfuls of cold water.

She drove very slowly; the narrow roads weren't gritted and she kept a tight grip on the steering wheel going downhill. The dual carriageway to Caernarfon was gritted, but here, too, the few cars she saw were crawling along, as if everyone expected it to start snowing again at any moment. I mustn't bask in the security, she thought. Curling up by the stove. Allowing him to take charge. Letting the dog lick my hand. She pulled over in a lay-by and got out of the car without putting on her coat. She dragged herself over a fence, walked a good distance through the snow, then turned round. She looked at her footsteps, she looked at the car, she shivered. This is it, she thought. This is the situation. Her shoes were wet, her toes cold. An empty car by the side of the road, bare trees, hills, cold. A badger that no longer appears; standing in a pond with water up to my waist, no heavy objects in my pockets. The smell of an old woman in my body. This is it. This is the situation.

42

Once again, there was no one in the waiting room, which was immediately inside the front door. No receptionist; a bell announced that someone had come in. She sat down on one of the four chairs and waited. After about five minutes, when she still hadn't been called in, she lit a cigarette. She couldn't hear any voices on the other side of the surgery door. Now and then people walked past the window, looking in inquisitively. There was a clean ashtray and a pile of magazines on a Formica coffee table.

'Ah, the badger lady.'

She looked up and sighed.

'Don't be so dismissive,' the doctor said. 'I'm only joking. Come in.'

His desk was empty, there were no documents he had just been working on. She was already so used to people here smoking almost everywhere that she hadn't stubbed her cigarette out in the waiting room. She did it now, in his half-full ashtray. She looked at the cross, which someone had straightened.

'Your hair's nice like that. A bit on the short side.'

'Thank you.'

'Shirley is a very experienced hairdresser. What's more, she's the last hairdresser.'

She looked at him.

'So you thought it was necessary now?'

'What?'

'Coming to see me.'

'Yes.'

'What can I do for you?'

'Painkillers.'

'You can get them at the chemist's. You don't need me for that.'

'I'm not talking about aspirin or paracetamol.' That last word sounded strange. She wasn't sure it was English.

'What *are* you talking about?'

'That's for you to say. I have no idea.'

'Sit down over here first. I need to look at your foot.'

'There's nothing wrong with my foot. Not any more.'

'Please.'

I mustn't be difficult, she thought. It can't do any harm. She sat on the bed and took off her wet shoe and sock. The skin of her foot was wrinkled. I could just lie down, she thought. Lie down and surrender and see what happens.

The doctor took hold of her foot. 'That's healed beautifully. Has it given you any more trouble?'

'No. Baking soda does wonders. You were absolutely right.' She stared over the doctor's shoulder at the wall. Only now did she realise – perhaps because it was lit from a different angle or because she was now looking at it without really focusing – that the HIV poster showed the torso of a dark-skinned man. Not from the front, but from the side, soft focus, a pert arse. Only now did she understand the 'Exit Only' at the bottom. The poster must have been ancient. She wondered why *this* man had a thing like *that* hanging in his surgery. She couldn't imagine it striking a chord with many patients in this small town.

The doctor held her hand and felt her pulse with two fingers. 'Hmm,' he said. He took her head between his hands, raised the skin above her eyes with his thumbs and looked into her eyes carefully. Then he ran one hand down her arm, while laying his other on her knee. If I were a non-smoker, she thought, his breath would be incredibly foul. 'Headache?' he asked.

'Yes.'

'Is that all?'

'No.'

'What else seems to be the problem?' The bell rang in the waiting room. He glanced at the door and took advantage of the interruption to cough, without raising a hand to his mouth.

She slid down off the bed, standing up against him for a brief instant before he took a step back. There was some forgotten stubble on the Adam's apple in his scrawny neck. For someone who had just laid a hand on her knee, almost like Sam resting his head there, he jumped out of the way extremely quickly. She sat down on the chair and lit a cigarette. For the first time, she felt she had the measure of this man.

The doctor sat down too and wasn't going to be outdone.

Together they sat there smoking. 'You do realise that I can't prescribe strong analgesics just like that?'

'I don't see why not.'

'There *is* such a thing as a medical code of ethics.'

'That didn't seem to bother you very much the other day in the hairdressing salon.'

'Aha. You think I shouldn't talk to Shirley about my patients? That's not the same as prescribing medicine without a reason.'

'Without a reason? Who said that?' She blew a cloud of smoke in his face.

The doctor blew a cloud back. 'Then I'll ask again, what's the problem?'

'I'm ill.'

'How ill?'

'I don't know.'

'You're not being treated? In Holland?'

'Of course.'

'So why won't you tell me what it is?'

'It's none of your business.'

'I'm a GP. I have to abide by rules and I have a conscience.'

'I'm a coincidental patient. I might leave again for Holland in the morning. That business with the badger was an incident. I'm a tourist.'

'Where's the pain?'

'Everywhere. Sometimes it's like toothache through my whole body.'

'Toothache?'

'As if you go to the dentist because of the pain and you think you know where it is and the dentist goes to work on a completely different tooth, which surprises you, but the next day the pain is gone.'

'Hmm.'

'I smell things too.'

'That can only be healthy.'

'No. Things that aren't there. Or things I imagine and then I really smell them.'

The doctor let that go by. 'If I prescribe this medication for you . . .'

She looked at him and tried to guess what he was suggesting. 'I'm a tourist,' she said again. 'I'm here by coincidence alone. I could have gone to a doctor in Bangor just as easily.'

'I can't allow this.'

She gestured at the ashtray, now more than half full. 'What are you doing?'

'Sorry?'

'You're sitting here smoking yourself to death under a cross and a poster of a bare black arse. You even joke about it. Is no one stopping you?'

He looked at the wall. 'I don't quite under—'

'Doesn't it matter, your smoking? Is it irrelevant?'

His Adam's apple bobbed up and down. 'My wife complains about it.' He cleared his throat, then started coughing.

'But you don't let her stop you?'

'No. Is anyone stopping you?'

'No. I'm alone. Completely alone. Did you make a record of my last visit?'

'Of course.'

'Destroy it. Forget that I'm here now.' She didn't take her eyes off him. 'Is my name on it?'

'No.'

The doctor didn't look away. He pulled on his cigarette, which was burnt down almost to the filter, and stared at the ashtray. From the waiting room came the sound of someone moving a chair, clearly audible. He dropped the butt in the ashtray without stubbing it out. Then he opened a drawer and, after shuffling papers and searching, removed a form that he folded twice before tearing it into shreds. The shreds disappeared in the waste-paper basket. He took a pen and began to write a prescription. 'You know where the chemist is. I'll give you this, but then I don't want to see you here again, ever.'

'The strongest there is.'

Without looking up, he screwed up the piece of paper and wrote a new prescription, which he held out to her. 'I don't know you,' he said.

There was a woman in the waiting room. A woman with bleached hair pinned up on top of her head. It looked very thin in the light of the fluorescent lamp. She was leafing through an ancient magazine. 'Hello, love,' she said.

Shirley, she thought. If I'd been forced to make up a name for her, it's the name I'd have chosen. 'Good morning.'

'Don't be so formal! How do you like your new hairdo?'

'I'm sorry?'

'Your hair? How do you like it?'

'What about my hair?'

'I cut it just the other day.'

'I've always worn my hair like this.'

The hairdresser gaped at her.

'Free consultation?' she asked.

'What?'

'I beg your pardon, I thought you were someone else.' She opened the door and stepped out onto the snowy pavement. Carefully she shuffled towards the chemist's. There were almost no lights on in the hairdressing salon, only the lamps around one of the four mirrors. The door was not ajar. The perfumery across the road had a large sign in the window announcing a sale with 50 per cent discount on all items. *One day there'll be nothing but badgers walking around this town. People have already started to go away.* She heard the man she no longer knew saying it. *Or they simply die, that's an option too of course.* The chemist's was open. There were even customers waiting at the counter. They weren't holding a sale here.

The young man who served her peered at the prescription for a long time and then looked up, probably to ask why the patient's name was missing. She stared at him the way she had just stared at the hairdresser and he went into the back room. Once she had her plastic bag of tablets, she walked back to the car park on the other side of the road. It occurred to her that, as far as the boy was concerned, her hair had always been like this. He didn't know her any other way. Neither did the dog that apparently saw her as a fellow canine. In the window display of an outdoor shop, the shop where she'd bought the map, there were male heads wearing woolly hats. One of them, bearing the brand name Patagonia, was pastel blue with an edge in various other shades of blue, from very light to very dark, like a bar code. It made her think of the mountain and what the boy had said yesterday morning. She'd heard him, she just hadn't responded. She went into the shop, bought the hat and asked the shop assistant to gift-wrap it, watching while he fiddled awkwardly with a roll of Sellotape. A muscle in her right leg quivered. She felt hot. The hat was expensive. That doesn't matter, she thought, I don't have to worry about that. She said goodbye to the shop assistant – who looked at her with surprise – and left. It wasn't until she was outside that she worked out what had happened. She must have said it in Dutch, '*Tot ziens*', even though she was sure she was speaking English. The clock on the arch in the town wall said quarter past eleven.

43

The boy wasn't home. She laid the hat under the Christmas tree, which was standing in the corner next to the sideboard, already hung with tinsel and baubles and with the fairy lights on. He'd put it in a zinc tub with a load of crushed slate to weigh it down. She climbed the stairs slowly, pushed open the bathroom door, laid the tablets on the shelf above the washbasin and took one without reading the leaflet. The doctor hadn't quibbled on quantity. The tubes of cough drops were on the shelf too, unopened. She sat down on the toilet. The cramp she had felt in the car came back. And again. Each time she went to tear off some toilet paper, she had to pull her hand back. 'Goodness,' she said quietly, elbows on her knees, her head hanging down over the tiled floor. After wiping her bottom, she ran the bath for the second time that day, again adding a good squirt of Native Herbs. The bubble bath had a pungent smell. A real smell. She took off her clothes and sat down in the hot water, thinking about the boy's monologue and all the things he'd reeled off smoothly, as if he had thought about it beforehand, as if there were a plan behind it. She tried to feel what the tablet was doing inside her body by imagining the journey the active ingredients were making from their starting point in her stomach. Hopefully reaching her head sometime soon. When a pleasurable lethargy began to seep through her, she realised that it would soon be New Year.

'Hello!' That wasn't Bradwen, if only because he would have turned it into a question. Rhys Jones. Already through the front door, and her in the bath. The front door led straight to the stairs. In this house, climbing them was a completely natural thing to do. She had to get out of the bath; the door wasn't even locked. The water splashed loudly. The tablet had done its job: it was her own body that got out of the bath, but with a slight lag. She hadn't heard a car. She took the towel from the hook on the door and pressed it against her breasts. He knocked on the door, fairly hard. 'Go away,' she said. In the silence that followed, she leant her head on the wooden door panel. She thought she could hear him breathing and at the same time she heard the baker's wife saying something. *And if she was still alive she would never have let him eat so much cake.* If only she were standing at the baker's now, fully dressed, with hiking boots on her feet. The bathwater was still settling. It was very clear.

'I'll wait in the kitchen.'

She recoiled from his voice, which resonated in the wood. She heard him go downstairs. Slowly she dried herself, leaving the plug in the bath; the gurgling water would make too much noise. Slowly she pulled on her clothes. Cramps in her belly that didn't really hurt, no pressure behind her ears, a numbness in her head. Before opening the door, she looked out of the small window at the snow-covered drive. What was keeping Bradwen? The geese were huddled together in front of the shelter. In front of it, never inside it. Stupid animals.

Rhys Jones was sitting on the kitchen chair closest to the Christmas tree, the gift-wrapped hat in his hands. There was something about him, something different.

'What are you doing?' she asked.

'I assume you don't put presents under the tree for yourself.'

'And?'

'I was imagining you'd bought this for me.'

'What?'

'Who else comes to visit you?' He squeezed the parcel. 'It feels like socks.'

'Put it back.'

'It's not for me?'

I could grab a knife, she thought. The heavy frying pan if necessary. 'No.'

'You are living here alone, after all? Isn't that what you told the agent when you signed the provisional rental agreement?' He laid a special emphasis on the word 'provisional'.

'Mr Jones.'

'Call me Rhys.'

'Mr Jones, would you be so kind as to put that package back?'

'Fine, fine, be as uppity as you like.' He stood up and returned the hat to its place under the tree. He straightened his back, turned round and went into the living room. She heard the front door open.

She looked around. The kitchen was safe for a moment. The three flowering plants on the windowsill, the coffee pot on the cooker, the Christmas tree. She still had a quick look in the cutlery drawer, at the biggest compartment. The front door closed. Rhys Jones came into the kitchen carrying a plastic crate. She looked at his feet and, while looking down, realised what was different about him: his thick greasy hair was a good bit shorter, she'd seen his ears for the first time.

'Lamb,' he said, putting the crate on the table.

She looked into it. A few hunks of dark-coloured meat. She raised a hand to her throat. 'Is that a whole lamb?'

'No. A half of lamb.'

'A half?'

'I was only going to give you a quarter, but that would have been leaving you with hardly any. I'm a soft touch.' And as he said that, he put a hand on her bum, as if to prove it.

She didn't grab the hand; it was the one with the torn

fingernail. Instead she stepped aside, as calmly as possible, away from the hand, and kept moving. She ended up directly opposite on the other side of the table. 'Take it away again.'

'Isn't it good enough for you?'

'What do you want?'

'I've brought you a couple of legs of lamb. Completely free of charge.'

'I don't want them. Lamb disgusts me.'

'Too bad. I'm leaving it anyway. I've fulfilled my obligations.'

'You can leave, then.'

'You look very different from last time,' he said.

'You can leave, then.'

'Have you been to the hairdresser's? Shirley's?'

She had put her hands on the back of a chair. Shirley, the doctor, the man opposite her, the baker and his wife; everyone knew each other. Everyone except Bradwen. He was the only one who didn't fit in. What was keeping him? Although, having decorated the Christmas tree first, he could be gone for a while yet. She looked at the clock. Almost half twelve. I have to do something, she thought. It doesn't matter what. She went through to the living room, opened the door of the stove, pushed two logs onto the smouldering fire, and slid them back and forth a little with the poker. She realised that she was standing with her back to Rhys Jones, bent forward. She felt strong.

The sheep farmer had followed her and was now sitting sprawled on the sofa with one arm on the backrest. 'Don't I get any coffee?' he asked. 'Badger lady?'

'What did you say?'

'I said, badger lady.'

'You're not getting any coffee. You can leave now.' She stayed where she was, next to the stove, without putting the poker back in the wood basket.

'My estate agent friend rang up.'

She looked at his socks.

'They've tracked down a great-nephew. Lives in England. Your tenancy won't be renewed.'

She moved the poker to her other hand.

'Seeing as my friend's a nice guy, he realises that it's very short notice and he's giving you until 5 January to pack your stuff. We'll be dropping by on New Year's Day, though, to check the condition of the house.'

'No problem.'

'No?'

'No. None of this old junk is mine. I don't need a moving van.' She looked out of the window. It was as if she sensed that would be the second in which Bradwen would come over the garden wall. He didn't jump this time, he climbed. Sam jumped, landing next to the oak and alder branches. Apparently he remembered exactly where they were. Strange he's coming from that direction, she thought. The boy walked across the snowy lawn and stopped at the edge of the dug-up section. She wondered if he could see her. The living room was fairly gloomy with its single window but, as ever, the standard lamp was on. Bradwen gave the dog a command. Sam turned back and sat down against his leg, partly hidden by the rose bushes. Why is he standing there? she thought. Can he see Rhys Jones's car from there? And what of it?

'You'll have enough time to eat the legs of lamb.'

'I don't eat lamb.'

'Please yourself. Mrs Evans loved lamb. She made it to ninety-three on it.' He looked up. 'What are you doing over there? Come and sit on the sofa.'

'It's time for you to leave,' she said. 'You've fulfilled your obligations and you've delivered your message.'

'I still haven't told you how Mrs Evans met her end.'

'I'm not interested. I didn't know the woman.'

'I think you'd find it very interesting.'

From the corner of her eye she saw Bradwen still standing in the same spot. She shook her head, wondering if the man on the sofa could really have such primitive thought processes. He's a widower, she seems to be unattached. *What's holding us back?* The boy moved an arm. Was he reacting to the shake of her head? She raised the poker, without knowing what exactly she wanted to indicate. 'Cigarettes,' she said.

'What?'

'In the kitchen. My cigarettes.' It annoyed her that she hadn't just gone to the kitchen without a word. The kitchen in the house that was hers until 5 January. She went to the window and gestured to Bradwen that she would come out, laid the poker on the table and lit a cigarette. Then she went straight to the front door and opened it. That was too much for Sam. He jumped up, barked and ran towards her. The boy let the dog go; he didn't call him back.

Rhys Jones rose from the sofa with surprising speed. 'Sam?' he said.

The dog swerved slightly, ran to the sheep farmer and jumped into his arms.

Rhys Jones staggered.

She looked at Bradwen. Then back at the sheep farmer, whose eyes seemed even moister than usual.

Sam snorted and licked and barked.

44

'*S'mai, Dad*,' said Bradwen.

Rhys Jones put the dog down without answering the greeting. 'Stay,' he said. His galoshes were on the doorstep, facing away from the house; he could step right into them. He did, keeping his balance with one hand on the jamb. The dog looked up at him, panting excitedly. Without so much as looking at Bradwen, he walked down the crushed-slate path to his car, which was parked next to the house with the bumper almost touching the old pigsty. He opened the car door. 'Sam,' he called. The dog – which had tried to peer round the corner, nervous, with his head at an angle – flew out of the house and leapt into the car without a moment's hesitation; it was obviously something he'd done many times before.

She had come out too by now, in her socks. A kind of triangle resulted: Rhys Jones at the car, Bradwen next to the future rose bed and her at the door. It wasn't really cold any more; the last flakes of snow were dripping from the rose leaves.

'So those socks are for you?' the sheep farmer said. It

wasn't really a question. He'd already gone round the car and opened the door on the driver's side.

'Socks?' the boy asked.

She looked from the boy to the man and back again. If Bradwen is a gymnast, she thought, Rhys Jones is a judoka who gave it up twenty years ago and let himself go to seed. She sucked on her cigarette, very hard, and blew out the smoke, which was thick in the damp air. Rhys Jones climbed in and started the car. Sam sat next to him, alert and staring straight ahead, his tongue lolling out of his mouth. A sheepdog. Happy. Next to his real master, the alpha male. Suddenly she understood why the dog had sat with her so often, why he had so willingly abandoned his post in front of the bathroom door that very first day: she was on the same level as the boy. The black car – it *was* a pickup – backed up, disappearing from her field of vision. She saw the shelf under the mirror before her, the first box of tablets. Just as her own body had seemed to emerge from the water with a slight lag earlier, everything outside seemed to be a quarter of a second out of sync too. She wanted to take another tablet now to keep it that way.

Shirley, the doctor, the baker and his wife, Rhys Jones *and* Bradwen. The boy was very naked now, without a dog, behind the pots with scrawny, dripping rose bushes, the straps of a small rucksack across his chest. 'Come here,' she said, when the car was out of earshot. If she didn't call him, he would probably just stay there. She tossed the cigarette away and grabbed the boy. The rucksack was in the way; she wormed her hands in under it and hugged him to her chest. He smelt unbelievably good.

She let her hands slide down and pulled his lower body up against hers.

'Socks?' he asked again, warm breath on her throat. He had wrapped his arms lightly around her.

'That man doesn't know what he's talking about,' she said. She saw the oak lying there like a fallen candelabra with uneven arms. If the tree's left to lie there like that, it will end up turning into a second moss bridge. The smell of fresh bread overwhelmed the smell of the boy.

45

The husband moved his leg. That was what it felt like. Before, he'd only had to move his foot, but in the last few days the plaster cast had grown heavier and his leg cumbersome. Unable to drive, he'd taken a no. 4 tram to De Pijp, where he had arranged to meet the policeman in the bar on the Van Woustraat. He was glad he didn't have to go to his parents-in-law's by himself. Between the bar and their house the snow hadn't been cleared off the pavement and the streets hadn't been gritted; the policeman had to save him from falling more than once. The TV was on – long-distance ice skating – the commentators' voices were a mumble in the background. One of the skaters was the one he'd seen advertising bread on the poster at the tram stop. His father-in-law was making tea; the policeman preferred it to coffee. Next to the TV was a Christmas tree decorated with tinsel and candles. His parents-in-law liked to do things the old-fashioned way and didn't light the candles until Christmas Day itself. The triangle on the windowsill *was* lit, the flames adding an orange tint to a white amaryllis.

'How'd they figure that out?' the father asked.

'No idea. "That information is confidential." That's what the woman who phoned me said.'

'A woman?'

'Yes.'

'Wales. How'd she end up there? What's in Wales?'

'An English-speaking country's an obvious choice, of course.'

'And what's it got to do with you?'

The policeman glanced at the husband before answering. 'He can't drive,' he said, gesturing at the cast. 'I've got some time off saved up. If I don't use it before the end of the year, I lose it.'

'When are you going?'

'Next week.'

'For Christmas?'

'Yep. It's Christmas everywhere.'

'Don't you have a wife? Kids? How do they feel about it?'

'Oh, it's fine by them,' the policeman said. 'They're used to me being on duty.'

'Hmm,' said the father.

'Unbelievable,' said the mother.

'What?'

'That Kramer's a monster. He's even accelerating.'

'Did you hear a word we said?'

'What do you think? I was never really worried.'

'Well, I was.' He poured them all a second cup of tea. 'I've had to take valerian at night,' he told the policeman. 'I could barely sleep otherwise.'

'That's good stuff,' the policeman said. 'I take it too sometimes.'

'Do you?'

'Have you been in touch with her?' the father asked.

'No. I wouldn't know how,' the husband said. 'I still haven't been able to get through on her mobile.'

'But you've got her address?'

'Yes. Kind of. I've got the name of a house.'

'Then you could send her a letter.'

'I could.' The husband watched the TV for a moment. 'It really is unbelievable, them tracking her down.'

'That's what they do,' the policeman said.

The husband stood up. 'I'll just go to the loo,' he said, grabbing a crutch and hobbling from the living room out into the small hallway. In the toilet he closed the lid and, after some effort, managed to sit down. With the door shut, he didn't really have enough room for his foot. He couldn't think about his wife in the living room and he had to decide what to say to his parents-in-law. Whether to tell them. Strange people, totally impervious. The way his father-in-law had just told the policeman about taking valerian to get to sleep. His mother-in-law nursing the exercise book she used to jot down the lap times. He wondered how long it was since he'd written a letter and realised how old-fashioned all that was: a pen, paper, envelope, stamp, postbox. His armpit was a bit chafed where the policeman had gripped him those three or four times. He turned the tap on and then off again. He couldn't think about his wife here either. He found it completely impossible to imagine her in a house in the country.

A lot had changed in the last two months. Being alone didn't even feel strange any more. After a couple of days at home with his foot up on a stool and a beer within reach, he had called the practice. They wouldn't tell him anything. He'd sworn at them, and they'd put him through to the doctor. She too had kept silent and remained icy calm. He asked her about the results of the fertility test, something he'd completely forgotten during his visit. They were confidential too. Just before he rang off, she'd asked him how his foot was. That made him laugh out loud and he was still laughing when he hung up on her. He didn't know anything. There was nothing he could really tell his parents-in-law. He hauled himself upright.

'You were gone a long time,' the mother said.

'Yeah.' He gestured at the cast.

'We're so happy. Really, very happy,' the father said. 'That she's been found.'

'Shouldn't we open a bottle of something?' the mother asked. The skating was finished, there were commercials on TV, the sound was turned right down. She'd laid the exercise book on the windowsill.

'Good idea. Help yourself to a glass of white,' the father said. 'The bottle's in the fridge. It needs using up.'

'Men? A drop of genever?'

'Sure,' said the policeman.

Men, thought the husband. *A drop*. 'I'll have one too while you're at it.'

'Could you slice up a dried sausage?' the father said to the mother's back. 'Was it expensive?'

'Yes,' said the husband. 'Very.'

The father looked at him. The husband thought he was going to offer to pay a share of the investigation fee. Instead the father turned his attention to the policeman. 'How come you didn't put him in prison?' he asked.

'Because he's such a nice guy.'

'You misinformed me,' the policeman said. They were negotiating the slippery pavement on their way back to the Van Woustraat. After two shots it seemed a lot easier.

'I know,' the husband said. 'They're a strange couple.'

'Things like that have a knock-on effect.'

'What do you mean?'

'I could start questioning the truth of what else you've said.'

'You're not a detective, are you?'

'No, I'm just a simple police officer. But I'm also human.'

The husband's crutches slipped out from under him – he had to put his cast down on the ground. He didn't fall over – the policeman already had him in a firm grip.

'Never,' the policeman said. 'You can never tell exactly what someone's thinking or feeling.'

'You want to eat?' the husband asked. 'I haven't got anything at home.'

'OK,' the policeman said. 'There's a Turkish place just up the road. You can make it that far.'

'Can you just stay away like that? What will your wife think? Won't your kids miss you?'

The policeman smiled.

I need a kind of shoulder pad, thought the man, but in my armpit. An armpit pad. He'd got into a good rhythm, pushing the crutches deep into the snow. I could send a card with a priority sticker on it. Old-fashioned, but the only way.

46

She tore off chunks of bread and threw them to the geese. Three birds ate the bread, a fourth watched her every move. There was hardly any snow left, the land was steaming. Between the trunks of the oaks in the wood behind the goose shelter it was already growing dark. A few sheep stood around the hay, most of the others were grazing. 'Strange,' she said. 'At first they disappeared really quickly and now these four have been left for quite a while.'

The boy didn't speak.

'They're not anybody's. What if I just left?'

'I'd still be here.'

'Yes,' she said slowly. 'You'd still be here.'

The boy cleared his throat.

She looked left. A sound she'd heard before was coming from the oak wood, but she didn't recognise it until the big brown bird took off from a branch.

'A kite!' Bradwen said.

'A bird,' she said.

It swooped low over the ground and, like the last time,

glided up to disappear over the roof ridge of the house, which it seemed to use as a kind of ski jump. It made the geese restless.

'It's a red kite.'

She couldn't work it out. She knew that it meant something else, this word that the boy had said twice now, but she could only picture a red diamond on a string with a tail of knotted rags. Somewhere in her head, something needed to happen. His English needed to become her English, so that she could simply understand him. '*Vlieger*,' she said.

'What?'

'*Vlieger*. I don't understand what you're saying.'

'I don't understand what you're saying.'

Her left temple started to pound. She wanted to say 'kite', she was sure of that, her tongue was definitely moving towards the roof of her mouth, slightly to the back, but instead she blew air out between her lower lip and upper teeth and her tongue relaxed, not altogether involuntarily, and came to rest where the roof of her mouth met her teeth. Bradwen began to say incomprehensible things, spitting out sounds. She looked him in the eye, fixing on his squint in the hope that he might somehow be able to explain things to her in some other way, without words, without sounds.

'There, there.' That she understood. His arms around her belly as if he were scared that something would fall out, that too was familiar. His breath on the back of her neck. The geese acted like they weren't seeing anything. They were whiter again, their beaks brownish now, not the bright orange they'd been in the snow. Please go inside for

[148]

once, she thought. The sheep were almost invisible. Her hands on the top board of the gate. As if she were pushing against it with the boy holding her back. If someone came down the path now, they might think he was raping her. Had the English named man-made kites after that big brown bird? she wondered, and now its Dutch name came to her. The *wouw*, red or otherwise. He's not raping me, she thought. He's taking care of me. He's a sweet boy. A beautiful gymnast. And he should have left long ago.

'I need a tablet,' she said.

'What kind of tablet?'

'A tablet the doctor prescribed for me this morning.'

'In Caernarfon?'

She could stand again. She could talk to him normally again.

The boy rubbed her tummy with his lower arms, still breathing on her neck. Not just a boy now, a son.

'There's one thing I want to know,' she said.

'Yes?'

'This afternoon or this morning, I've forgotten which . . .' I really have forgotten, she thought. Maybe it's the next day already? She looked at the steaming countryside. Where had the snow got to so quickly?

'Yes?'

Not the next day then? 'Why did you come over the stream and the garden wall?'

'I took a detour via the stone circle.'

'What for?'

'To have a look. There was snow. If there'd been tracks, I would have seen them.'

'And?'

'Nothing.'

No badgers. No fox. No dog. It was a shame that Sam was gone. If he hadn't driven off with the sheep farmer, he could have leant against her legs now, or against the gate, to get at her hands. To lick them. The hands of the alpha female.

47

Buying, writing and sending a card was hardly straightforward. Just choosing one, for starters. The local Bruna had seven revolving racks full of them. The shop was incredibly busy too; he had to deploy his crutches – 'Careful, Josje, that man wants to get past!' – to reach them. Everything had significance, she could read something into every picture. In the end it came down to a choice between a hippo and a dog. He pulled the card with the dog out of the rack, mainly because she'd never been crazy about pets and could misinterpret the hippo. A neutral card. He'd already started to pay when he remembered stamps and priority stickers.

The student. She had told him herself, very coolly. Here in this living room, on a Sunday evening. He'd just got back from a run and was about to shower. It had been over for ages, she said. It was the real reason she'd been fired. During his run, he'd smelt the change of seasons and looked forward to competing in drizzle. The autumn races. Still sweating and with his chest expanded, he had stood there in the living room. Her confession was matter-of-fact; he had listened calmly. Now he knew that there was something else she had kept quiet. They had spent a week avoiding each other, then she'd disappeared. Two days later, he noticed an empty spot in the living room. After doing a circuit of the house and discovering that other things were missing too, he went through her desk drawers and found a number of notes: *Our 'respected' Translation Studies Lecturer screws around. She is in no way like her beloved Emily Dickinson. She is a heartless Bitch*. He went looking for her. He visited his parents-in-law and drove to the university. In a corner he found one more note and then he knew for certain that they had been hung all over the building. In her office, which was empty but unlocked – trusting people, academics – he had finally imagined this student, a boy whose name he didn't even know, who had probably been there in that very place, maybe with his jeans down around his ankles. That image got to him. Not an image of his wife, no, the boy. Without being fully aware of what he was doing, he had torn up a couple of books and hurled them under a desk. With a box of matches he'd found in a pen tray, he'd initiated a book-burning. When it got out of hand – he felt the heat of the flames on his face – he opened the door and shouted, 'Fire!' He was confused, definitely, but he wasn't a pyromaniac.

He stared at the dog on the card for a long time. It wasn't going to tell him what to write. A group of cyclists rode by, giggling girls, wobbling across the full breadth of the road, mobile phones at the ready. Ring-necked parakeets squawked in the small park on the edge of his neighbourhood. Being at home alone wasn't unpleasant. There was a glass of red wine in front of him on the coffee table. He felt calmer, more at ease. From the Bruna, he'd hobbled to the flower stand, where he'd bought a large bunch of yellow tulips. Not Christmas but spring. The spring races were beautiful too; he'd have to concentrate on them now. He saw himself going out the door alone, returning alone, no hellos or goodbyes, no sighs. He'd already addressed the envelope and stuck two stamps on it; in the shop he hadn't thought about the difference between domestic and European. Now he just had to write something. What did he want to say to her? If he was very honest, not much. 'I'm coming,' he wrote, with her name above it and his underneath. He quickly slipped the card into the envelope and licked it shut. Then he drained the glass and called the policeman.

48

The ease with which Bradwen once again used the hotplates and the oven made her realise that he must have been familiar with the cooker for a long time. He had slid a leg of lamb into it – with garlic and anchovies, as promised – but he could eat it himself. The thought alone made her feel sick. Where had he got that tin of anchovies? Had he bought it earlier? She lit a cigarette. He must have seen the present under the Christmas tree. Maybe he was looking forward to it, just as she had always stared greedily at the St Nicholas presents in the old days but had to wait until someone told her that she could take one and unwrap it. She used to kill time by staring out of the window with feigned indifference. She smacked her lips, there was something strange about the taste of the cigarette. As long as she kept quiet, he couldn't do anything.

'Plant the roses tomorrow?' he asked.

'Yes, fine.'

He sat down at the table, a bit lost.

'Or maybe wait a little longer,' she said.

'It must have been Sam,' the boy said. He had clasped his hands loosely and was rubbing one thumb with the other in turn.

'What?'

'Foxes smell a dog.'

She tried to cast her mind back. Ten geese, eight geese, seven geese. She saw herself kneeling in the dark, chips of slate pressing into her flesh. There were four or five around then, but the boy and the dog hadn't arrived yet. Or had they? 'Do you know the baker and his wife?'

'Yes.'

'Why didn't you say so?'

'You didn't ask.'

'Don't they have a baker in Llanberis?'

'Sure. My father used to say he danced to the pipes of the tourists. Making rolls nobody else wanted. Fancy stuff.'

'So you don't have a mother any more.'

The boy bowed his head and looked down at his thumbs, dragging a nail through the wrinkles on his knuckle.

I didn't want to know a thing about him, she thought. He was just supposed to be here. But he had to leave too. And now I know he's a motherless son. That he left home and took his father's dog. She felt exhausted. She didn't want to know or hear any of the ins and outs. 'Pour a drink,' she said loudly.

The boy picked up the bottle she could have picked up herself and poured two full glasses. She raised hers, the boy raised his. She looked at him, he looked back. The kitchen smelt of meat. She raised her eyebrows.

'To the lamb,' Bradwen said.

'No.'

'To the roses?'

'Yes.' She drank.

The smell of lamb wasn't as bad as she'd expected; one and a half glasses of wine were enough to drown her slight sense of nausea. During the meal they hardly spoke. The boy ate a lot of meat. She watched him shovel it in and imagined a lamb with muscular buttocks, a bundle of vigour and vitality, gambolling over a hilly field. She understood why Bradwen was so wiry, strong and wiry, as robust as the meat he ate and had probably eaten throughout his childhood. Now and then she saw him glance at the Christmas tree, looking at the present he suspected to be socks. He no longer urged her to eat. He ate and drank. Once, he forgot that the dog wasn't there any more and whistled under his breath.

She shook her head. 'No,' she said. She was very tired. 'He's gone.'

*

When Bradwen had finished eating, he stood up to clear the table.

'Leave it,' she said. 'I'll do it in a minute. Look under the Christmas tree first.'

Without feigning surprise, he walked straight to the present, picked it up and came back to the table. 'Socks,' he said softly. It sounded reproachful, as if he was thinking of the encounter with his father. He laid the present on the table and pulled off the Sellotape before folding back the wrapping paper. He took the hat in his hands, looked up – his squint a bit more pronounced than usual – then pulled it down over his black hair.

She took a mouthful of wine and watched as the boy stood up and came round the table to kneel down next to her. She knew what he was going to do even before he, like Sam, began licking her free hand. She stared at his neck and the pastel-blue hat with the curls sticking out from under it, and from there her gaze moved to the candles on the windowsill, which had almost burnt down. There was still a large piece of lamb in the earthenware dish. She tried to think whether she knew any commands in English. What was she supposed to say? 'Down!' perhaps?

49

She woke in the night. The rushing of the stream was fairly loud, she'd slid the window up before going to bed. Was that what had woken her? Had the wind turned? She felt bloated, as if she'd eaten half a saucepan of potatoes and a whole plate of parsnips. There were noises from the bathroom. Bradwen was on the toilet. She struggled over onto her side and listened to the stream, imagining water flowing to the sea day after day, seawater evaporating, fresh water being drawn up from the salt, clouds floating to the land, rain falling on the mountain, water feeding the stream. A little later she realised that the boy wasn't *on* the toilet. He was probably kneeling in front of it. Retching. She sat up, throwing the covers aside. The bedroom was cold. She didn't just feel bloated, she felt terrible. So terrible she could hardly drag herself up onto her feet. The landing light was on, the bathroom door wide open. She walked there using the railing for support. Bradwen hadn't turned on the light in the bathroom itself and he wasn't kneeling, he was standing bent over and clutching the sides of the toilet bowl. His naked back was like a sick animal's, hunched but powerful, curved but taut. A gymnast. She had never seen him like this. She laid her right hand on his upper back and, without applying any pressure, moved it back and forth from shoulder to shoulder. 'There, there,' she said. She felt a wave forming under her hand, put her left hand on his stomach, imagining it more tanned than usual, the muscles tense, her little finger on the elastic of his underpants. It was as if she were the one who made sure he got rid of what needed to come up. He gagged and spewed, she felt his body relax. Never before had she felt this close to him. At the same time, holding him like this helped her stay upright.

'To think that your father's meat would make you this sick,' she said.

He coughed and spewed again. 'The meat?' he said.

'I didn't eat any.'

'Who's to say it wasn't your hand?'

She looked at the hand on his shoulder. No, she thought, it was the other one, the left hand that was now on his stomach. An infected hand? The boy stood up and wiped his mouth, shaking her off in the process. He stepped to one side, turned on the tap and began to brush his teeth. The light from the landing wasn't strong enough to see his face properly in the mirror.

'Just kidding,' he said after he'd rinsed his mouth.

'Yes, of course,' she said.

They were standing opposite each other, or more side to side. He took her hand and lifted it to his mouth. 'Just kidding,' he said again and kissed it. 'See you tomorrow.' He walked out of the bathroom and closed the study door behind him.

She couldn't see her own face properly in the mirror either. She licked the back of her left hand; it tasted like her. She took a tablet. Later, back in bed, the stream sounded more syrupy and when she imagined the water cycle again it was infinitely bigger, bluer, whiter and wetter. She laid her hands on her belly to have the boy with her, somehow, after all and even thought she could feel his tension radiating into her skin. How easy it would have been for her to let one hand descend a little, laying her other on his chest, pulling him back against her, his head on her shoulder, his throat defenceless, his smell mixed with a sour tang. Give and take, she thought, in the part of the imagined cycle where a cloud was about to rain on the mountain. Him behind me, me behind him. He has to go, but not entirely. 'There, there', and '*ach*', that's about all there is.

She drifted away on the syrupy flow of the stream, her thoughts stretching out, she was almost asleep. She had just enough time to think how pleasant that was, sleep. How separate from everything else. How free from the things that worry people when they're not sleeping, the things that scare them, the things that loom before them like a mountain.

50

'It must have been the anchovies,' Bradwen said, leaning on the rusty, broken-handled rake he was using to even out the soil he'd turned. He looked a little paler than usual, perhaps because of the hat. His own, old hat was dark green. Earlier in the morning, drinking a coffee, he hadn't taken the new one off. 'It was a tin I found in a kitchen cupboard. Who knows, it could have been there thirty years.'

She was leaning against the wall of the old pigsty. The sun was shining, there was hardly any wind. There was no longer any trace of snow or winter. Like before, she felt the warmth radiating from the light-coloured bricks. Like before, the smoke rose vertically from her cigarette.

'With her buying it long before I was born. That's a weird thought.'

She turned her head. There were no cows on the other

side of the garden wall. It felt lonely. A flock of raucous black birds – she didn't even try to name them, there were too many possibilities: crows, jackdaws, ravens or rooks – flew from one tree to the next. It was as if it only took them a minute to realise that a particular tree was unsuitable.

'Or is it impossible for something like that, in oil, to go off?'

He'd started to rake the second rectangle. The soil was light brown, it didn't look very rich. There wasn't a single ominous cloud. The geese, out of sight from where she was standing, clucked softly. Contented, not frightened. She *was* listening to him, but not everything he said was getting through. Maybe he was glad to be feeling better, relieved that he'd just managed a biscuit with his coffee. She felt no desire to answer. He was working, sweating, feeling healthy and alive. She drew on her cigarette, which she was holding between the fingers of her left hand, the hand which he – before coming up with the anchovy theory – had blamed, in jest or otherwise, for his vomiting. The old-woman smell was lingering around her again, or rather, still, even out here in the fresh air, despite the cigarette smoke. She threw away the butt and pulled open the door of the sty. There wasn't much wood left; the pile had shrunk without her noticing. For a while now the boy had been taking care of the stove and the fireplaces, along with going to Tesco's and the Waunfawr bakery. Apart from the doctor's visit, she had stuck close to the house. She'd come here and kept her world small, then she'd gone out – feeling homesick in the refrigerated aisle at Tesco's, walking to the bakery, having her hair cut short and standing in the reservoir – and now the world was limited again. The homesickness had subsided, almost unnoticed. The garden, the goose field, the house, her bed, the shelf under the mirror in the bathroom, the boxes of tablets. A whole life in a matter of months. Until the New Year. Because this house and garden weren't hers. It wasn't her shelf under the mirror. She was a tourist, a passer-by. A foreigner, a German according to most people here.

'I'm going to plant them,' Bradwen called.

She stared at the greenish tiles of the cellar floor. For a moment she imagined that, instead of Sam, it had been Bradwen sitting in the oafish sheep farmer's big black pickup. And that the dog was snuffling around here now.

'I want another arch,' she said. Now that the rose bushes were in the ground there was hardly anything to them. They'd looked a lot larger in the pots. 'Here, along the edge of the path, as a gateway to the side path. And then you have to buy two special roses. Roses that want to climb.'

'Ramblers,' the boy said.

'Is that what they're called? Take the car and drive to Dickson's Garden Centre.'

'Now?'

'Why not? I'll give you money.'

'OK.'

She pulled a hundred pounds out of her wallet and gave him the notes.

When he was gone, she took the lid off the bin, fished around inside and found the empty, greasy anchovy tin. She walked over to the window above the sink and, without too much difficulty, read *Best before: June 1984* on the bottom. The boy had even been right.

She looked up. From an invisible chimney, hidden between oak trees, smoke was rising as on a listless day in June – smoke from cooking, not heating – bees waltzed past the kitchen window, butterflies flitted from a red rose to a yellow rose; the garden wall was two stones higher, a farmer on a dull red tractor was tedding the grass and the alders along the stream were full and round. She had her hair up and she was wearing an apron. Maybe she was already widowed, maybe the man on the dull red tractor was Mr Evans and she was about to take him something. In a basket. She pressed up against the sink and considered adding some cold beer to the basket, two bottles, enough to make Evans feel drowsy, ready to let the grass be for a while and lie down under an oak. Stretching out in the shadows with her. Warm. Clothes off.

She threw the tin back into the bin and washed her hands with icy water. She pulled on her boots without tightening the laces. Then she went upstairs.

51

The portrait of Dickinson was facing the wall again. With a sigh she turned it round. For weeks the boy had been sleeping in the most beautiful room in the house, the only room with windows on two sides. 'Dual aspect,' the house-hunters on *Escape to the Country* would say content-edly. 'So light and bright and airy in here!' For weeks now the open volume of poetry had lain on the oak table with the blank sheets of paper next to it, pen and pencil waiting. Habegger's much-too-thick book didn't even mention the poem, let alone discuss it. Suddenly she was furious, not just at the biographer – the old gossip – but at Dickinson too. A puling woman who hid herself away in her house and garden, wordlessly insisting with everything she did and did not do that people should just ignore her, yet fishing for validation like a whimpering child, scared to death that the affection she showed others, mostly in letters, would remain unanswered. A bird of a woman who made herself small and can only have been fearful, signing letters 'Your Gnome', and staying timorously in her room during the memorial service in the entrance hall for her dead father, but keeping the door ostentatiously ajar to demand the lion's share of the attention for herself. 'I never was with any one who drained my nerve power so much. Without touching her, she drew from me. I am glad not to live near her,' wrote one of the men with whom she corresponded. A woman who took to wearing the white of a virgin. Only now did she realise that it had been this anger that had motivated her to write a thesis, subjecting what she saw as the many overrated poems to a critical investigation. Almost as a day of reck-oning. 'Not good,' she said softly. 'Not good at all.'

She picked up the biography and the *Collected Poems* and clomped down the wooden stairs in her boots. Before going out, she threw the biography in the bin on top of the empty anchovy tin. Even worse was that it still enraged her here and now. She laid the poems on the table, sat down on a chair and pulled her laces tight.

She crossed the stream, trying not to think of the distance she had to cover. Taking her own path step by step. She had pulled an alder branch out of the pile to use as a walking stick, one that came up to just past her waist, and now she swung it forward, put it down and swung it forward again. At the stiles she needed to use her hands more than ever: she didn't let go of the pole or the top board until she was standing on the ground on the other side. It was quiet in the oak wood, a thin mist rising from the lichen-covered trunks and branches. No animals anywhere. No cows, no sheep, not even grey squirrels. She could imagine squirrels hibernating; she could imagine any wild animal with a shaggy coat hibernating. She was getting hot. A familiar smell rose from the neck of her thick coat. The smell of old Mrs Evans.

At the stone circle she felt like sitting but decided to walk on. The rocks were dry; the lichen pale grey and brownish yellow. Around the gorse bushes there was a very vague smell of coconut. She followed the natural embankment between the tufts of stiff grass. There was no trace of the black cattle, she couldn't hear any birds. She was completely alone, as if she too were not there. She crossed the field to the reservoir, passing the standing stone, which she whacked with her stick. Today the water wasn't like a silver tray that had just been polished; an almost imperceptible breeze was rippling it. In the distance it was surging through the small brick building. She shuddered to think that not so long ago she had stood in this reservoir, seeing her body bent by the refraction of the light, air bubbles in her pubic hair, tiny fish around her toes. She walked to the big rock she had laid her clothes on last time, sat down and lit a cigarette. A car drove along an unseen road. She stirred the water with the stick, making wavelets that pushed out through the wind's ripples. She followed one until it died on the opposite bank. When she tried to suck on her cigarette, she noticed that her mouth no longer closed. She panicked, pushing her lower jaw up with her hand, but she still couldn't suck; it felt like the time an oral surgeon extracted a wisdom tooth from her upper jaw and left a hole that connected to the nasal cavity, breaking the vacuum you need to smoke. She threw the cigarette in the reservoir and breathed in deeply through her nose a couple of times, something she could only manage by pressing her tongue up against the roof of her mouth. Her tongue was still working and a little later she managed to close her mouth. She stood up, felt her knees wobble and, leaning heavily on the stick, walked towards the standing stone, where she rested, laying a hand on its cold top and looking at the trees lining the rolling field.

Before starting the climb, she imagined the dull red tractor with a shrewdly smiling Farmer Evans sitting on it. And chains, deep tracks in the grass. Maybe Mrs Evans – not yet widowed – had helped him to stand the stone upright, leaving the basket with the bread rolls, two pears and a bottle of lemonade at the water's edge. Maybe they'd laughed, run, rolled in the grass.

She hadn't wanted to know a thing. She'd resisted the temptation to look it up on the Internet. She'd left. Like an old cat that wants to be left in peace. Not that she'd ever experienced anything like that herself; they'd never had a cat in the narrow house in De Pijp. Her uncle had cats. 'If they're gone, they're dead,' he said and her aunt nodded. She looked back once again at the water and thought of him. Why didn't anyone ever say 'Go on. Go ahead'? Why had every last member of the kitchen staff done their best to get him out of the pond and into dry clothes, putting his shoes on the oven? To give him a chance to do a bit of carpentry? 'A wall unit,' she said and walked on.

By the time she reached the stone circle the second time, the light had changed. The gorse flowers were a darker yellow, the stiff grass a different green. She sat down on the big rock and dared to put a cigarette in her mouth, even though her hands were trembling and she dropped the lighter after lighting it. There was still an enormous silence. Badger lady without a badger, she thought. She felt her legs grow leaden, her back stiff, her arms heavy. It wasn't coming. Maybe it was hibernating. Aren't badgers a kind of small bear? Slowly she covered the last stretch to the house. She stood on the beams over the stream for a long time, looking at the water flowing downhill. It bubbled and foamed. Clear, ice-cold water.

52

Bradwen already had the arch in the ground. She stayed behind the wall for a few seconds in the spot he'd jumped over weeks before. That was very impressive of him, the wall came up to her chest. Was that the sound of him whistling contentedly under his breath? Sam's jump was even more impressive. She followed the path to the kissing gate near the old pigsty. The walk from the stone circle to the house had not entirely dispelled the heaviness and stiffness from her back and legs. Two ramblers were standing against a side wall; one of them had a flower.

Bradwen turned round. 'Look,' he said.

'Lovely. Excellent. I'll be right there.' She leant the alder branch against the wall next to the front door and went into the house. In the bathroom she shook all of the strips of tablets out of the boxes, washed one tablet down with a couple of mouthfuls of water, and went downstairs again. In the living room she pulled open the stove door and threw the boxes on the fire, not going out again until she'd watched them catch and burn. She thought of the prescription and saw the piece of paper sliding across the counter at the chemist's. There'd be a record of that somewhere, filed, but it didn't matter. It only had the doctor's name and address, not her name, and definitely not her address. The sun had disappeared; a red glow hung over the goose field. In half an hour it would be dark, maybe a couple of minutes later than yesterday, a virtually imperceptible difference. It was almost Christmas.

'Would you like to plant them?' the boy asked.

'OK.'

He walked to the shed, picked up the pots and pulled the rose bushes out by the stems. He had already dug two holes and partly filled them with compost. The bag lay under the arch on the slate path. 'Careful of the thorns.'

She lowered the first rambler into a hole and went to get down on her knees.

'Let me do that.' He was already squatting to fill the hole with compost, then stood to press it down firmly with his feet.

'You're not just a gymnast,' she said, 'you're a gardener too.'

'*Ach*, not at all. Anyone could do this. Have you been out for a walk?'

'Yes.'

'Here.' He gave her a few lengths of green string. 'If you tie this one up, I'll plant the other.'

She tied two branches to the arch and did the same on the other side after Bradwen had planted that one too. The single rose – off-white, more bud than flower – wobbled on a branch that was much too thin but didn't break off. The boy went inside and came out with a large saucepan. It was only when he held the pan at an angle next to one of the roses and water came pouring out that she realised what he was doing. He tossed the pan onto the grass, put his hands on his hips and sighed contentedly. 'It's time for your favourite programme,' he said.

'This ticks all the boxes!' exclaimed a spoilt bitch. Even though she and her equally spoilt husband had a budget of eight hundred thousand pounds, their house-hunting just wouldn't gel. He wanted 'contemporary' and she wanted 'character features'. Sort yourselves out, for God's sake, she thought, and don't bother us with it. 'This doesn't do it for me,' said the husband. 'Not at all.' She groaned. Bradwen brought her a glass of white wine without further comment. She didn't notice him until he was right next to her. He'd crept up on his L and R stockinged feet. Fish, she thought. He's taking good care of me. The boy crept back out of the room. He hadn't taken off his new hat. The right side of her face was glowing from the heat of the stove.

She slumped a little and leant her head back against the sofa. Although on TV they were now talking about a typical Victorian hallway, she saw Shirley's hairdressing salon before her: Rhys Jones waving his big hands to clear the cigarette smoke; the doctor in the cobalt-blue hairdresser's cape with bloodshot smoker's eyes and a strangely lecherous twist to his mouth; the hairdresser laughing so shrilly that her breasts jiggled and the tendons in her neck stood out obscenely; the house-and-garden magazines full of green pumpkins; and there's the door opening to let in the baker of all people, it's high time he had his hair cut too and his wife Awen pushes him in – her perm is sagging and a bit listless and it will be Christmas in a few days' time. The hairdressing salon has got very busy all of a sudden. A Border collie is lying under the magazine table; it licks one of the table legs, maybe another dog lay there not so long ago. There goes the telephone. Shirley answers and says, astonished, 'Yes, he is here. You must be psychic.' And Rhys Jones takes the handset for a short conversation with his estate agent friend, assuring him with a smile that the woman will leave the house and also telling him that he groped her, that she's got a 'glorious arse' and that she was only too keen to respond to his advances; a shame that she's leaving really and no one knows where. Strangely enough there's no cutting, washing or hairdrying going on. The word 'badger' crops up regularly and when it does they all laugh, except for the baker's wife and the dog, dogs don't laugh, and this dog seems to be trying to creep farther and farther away from the people. Near the door are plastic crates with big lumps of meat in them, watery blood trickling out over the tiled floor. Shirley asks the sheep farmer how his son is, what he's getting up to these days, and the sheep farmer turns pale, whistles his dog out from under the magazine table and almost slips over in the puddle of blood that's formed near the door. His dog starts to lick the tiles. 'Enjoy your lamb,' Rhys Jones says before banging the door shut behind him. Now she hears 'Emily' in the hairdressing salon. 'Emily.' It's unclear who's speaking. The doctor looks guilty and, like a bad actor, asks who they're talking about.

Bradwen was standing next to the sofa. 'Tea's ready,' he said, maybe for the second time.

On TV a team of clever people were competing in a quiz. Eggheads they called them here, even more mocking than *bollebozen* in Holland, the kind of people who did a PhD on someone like Emily Dickinson.

53

The boy had put new candles in the holders on the windowsill. There was a lit candle on the table too. Dickinson's *Collected Poems* lay next to her plate, shut. On the plate it was haddock again, with mashed potato and fennel. Colourless food.

She sat down and looked at him, thinking of the almost

subservient way he had worked for her an hour and a half ago. Stamping down the soil, pouring the water. 'Why haven't you gone away?' she asked.

'Who'd cook?'

'I can cook too.'

'Who'd plant the roses? Who'd do the shopping? Who'd keep the stove burning?'

'Why?'

The boy looked at her. The hat looked really good on him, even at the dinner table.

'Have you already brought in the pan?'

'No,' he said.

'Why?' she asked again.

'Do I ask you questions?' he said. 'Just look under the Christmas tree instead.'

She looked aside. A present was lying there. Before standing up to get it, she took a big mouthful of wine. She stayed next to the Christmas tree with Bradwen's gift in her hand.

'Socks,' she said softly.

The boy sniggered. 'That woman doesn't know what she's talking about.'

She tore off the paper. He had simply bought her a woolly hat. An incredibly ugly hat, purple, with sewn-on flowers in a range of colours, almost all of which clashed with the colour of the hat itself. A hippie hat, it even had two tassels hanging down the sides. She swallowed and was glad she was facing away from him. She swallowed again before pulling it on. It fitted perfectly. 'Just what I needed,' she said, turning and going back to the table.

Bradwen looked pleased and ate.

She drank and poked at the fish.

'What is it with this Dickinson?' he asked, gesturing at the poems with the mash-filled serving spoon.

'Yes. I wanted to ask you that too.'

'How do you mean?'

'Why do you keep turning her portrait round?'

'Those beady little eyes.'

'It's a photo.'

'So? She gives me the creeps. And you?'

'I was involved with her because of my work.'

The boy chewed. 'Hmm.'

'She had a dog too.'

'Yeah?'

'Yes, Carla.' She squeezed her lips into a circle between her thumb and index finger. It was called Carlo, the name was in her head, another detail that had angered her in Habegger's biography because the man only mentioned the dog four times. It was a Newfoundland, an enormous hairy beast – she had looked up a picture of the breed – and it was called Carlo. A timid little woman whose only friend was a big dog and Habegger didn't care. Now that she'd squeezed her lips into a circle, she tried it again. 'Carla.'

'A lapdog,' the boy said.

'No, a very large one.' She ran the back of her hand over her hot forehead and drained her glass of wine. 'Pour some more.'

Bradwen picked up the bottle obediently. 'Funny name for a big dog.'

'Yes.' Funny name for a big dog. She knew it meant

something, but translating it was somehow beyond her. She wanted to go upstairs to the shelf under the mirror. Not one, but two tablets. She stood up. She walked through to the living room and stairs. The boy didn't call after her. Without turning on the bathroom light, she grabbed the strips and dared to look at her backlit self. Fortunately she was wearing a hideous hat, a fancy-dress article, nothing anyone could take seriously. 'Carlo,' she said. 'Ohhhhh.' She saw her mouth open and close again: vague, colourless. The bathroom smelt of Mrs Evans, of course, as if she'd got out of the bath ten minutes ago and dried herself, leaning on the washbasin now and then with one hand. She swallowed the two tablets with a single mouthful of water. When she straightened up again, the two tassels swung cheerfully.

'You're not smoking,' the boy said. He had cleared the table, letting the food slide off her plate into the bin. Now he was washing up.

'What?'

'I haven't seen you smoking since this morning when I was doing the raking.'

She looked around. The packet of cigarettes wasn't on the table. She stood up slowly and rested on the back of the chair before moving farther.

'You don't have to,' he said without turning.

She picked up her coat, which was lying on the chair next to the sideboard, and felt the cigarettes in one of the pockets. The lighter wasn't in the other pocket. Now that she was standing next to the sideboard anyway, she turned on the radio. Music. There was something she wanted to do, something she had to do. She thought about it. From the sound of it, Bradwen was up to the cutlery, the crackling of burning wood came from the living room. The radio was turned down. Something. She'd already got rid of the tablet boxes. She thought hard and saw the lighter sliding out of her hand, heard it bounce off the rock with a dry click and land in the grass. 'Throw me those matches,' she said.

The boy took the box of matches from the windowsill and lobbed it over. She reached out to catch it, but was too sluggish or else the box was moving too fast. It bounced off the sideboard and landed on the floor near the Christmas tree. She bent over and fell. Immediately he was beside her.

'Don't worry,' she said. 'I'm OK.'

He took her by the hand and pulled her to her feet.

She sat down at the table and finally lit the cigarette. It was horrible, almost disgusting. As if she was fourteen again and smoking her first cigarette, a Camel non-filter her uncle had given her. That must have been one of the last times she was allowed to stay at his house. She coughed and tried again. Something that had tasted good for years couldn't suddenly turn disgusting, could it? Bradwen was still standing close by, at her elbow. The very idea of a cloud of smoke passing through her mouth and windpipe and into her lungs was so repulsive she couldn't inhale. She stubbed the cigarette out.

The boy coughed. Then asked, 'Coffee?'

'No.' She drained her glass, stood up and walked into the living room. She switched on the TV and sat down on the sofa. She heard him turn off the radio and go back to the washing-up. There was movement and noise in front of her, everything with a one-second delay. A wide ditch, more a canal really, a boat with two men in it. They pulled baskets out of the water and one of them contained an eel. They shook it out. Catches down 95 per cent since the replacement of the wooden lock gates, the fisherman explained. In the field next to the canal there was a solitary sheep. She stood up immediately and returned to the kitchen.

'Coffee after all?' the boy asked.

'No.' She went over to the freezer and pulled it open, removing the hunks of meat and putting them in the plastic crate that was still on the floor next to the freezer.

'What are you doing?'

She didn't answer, but picked up the crate and walked into the living room with it. The boy watched her every move like a dog. Ears pricked up, eyes alert, waiting for a command. She had to put the crate down to open the front door. It wasn't cold, even though there were no clouds. A vast sky hung over the house and garden. For the first few steps she had light, shining out through the kitchen window. Beyond that band of light, she stopped briefly to let her eyes adjust. The stream murmured and the crushed slate crunched under her bare feet. One by one, she took the stiff, frozen pieces of lamb out of the crate and hurled them into the water with all the strength she had. Each lump was as heavy as a rock; like rocks they would lie on the bed of the stream. Holding the empty crate loosely in one hand, she stared at the dark water in which the enormous sky slowly became visible. Giving up smoking, she thought to herself, that's something healthy people do. Walking back to the door, she saw the white rosebud grow lighter. Her head was warm. Maybe the hat was made of real wool. Sheep's wool.

After closing the front door, she heard Bradwen rummaging around upstairs. 'What's going on up there?' she called, wiping the grit off her feet.

Bradwen emerged from the study. 'I'm arranging the new bedroom.'

It was hard for her to look up after having looked down for a while.

'I've put your bed in front of the fireplace. I still have to light it.'

'And you?'

'On the divan as usual.'

'*Godnogaantoe*,' she swore softly, under her breath. Only now, after weeks and weeks living in this house, did she realise that the stove in the living room and the fireplace above it shared the same flue. 'After Christmas, you're gone,' she said.

'I don't think so,' he said, coming downstairs.

54

She woke up because the boy had laid two logs on the embers and needed to blow to get the fire going again. He crept back to the divan. Earlier he'd pushed both windows up a little. It was unbearable in the study otherwise.

'It was very different with Sam here,' he said.

She didn't answer, staring at the ceiling.

'Dogs like Sam can't sleep all night, they start to move around. He'd whimper and come and sniff at me.'

'He even went downstairs.'

'No, not that. He'd always stay here.'

She sighed, turning her head towards him. Bradwen was half under the duvet with his hands behind his head. 'What time is it?'

'No idea. Three-ish?'

Her whole body seemed to be full of heavy things: lead, concrete, oak beams. She didn't even want to try to turn over onto her side. She thought of the night Bradwen vomited, the idea that some part of the tension in his body had passed into hers through her hands. 'You're moving around too,' she said.

'Just now. The fire was almost out.'

No, her body itself was the heavy things: legs made of oak beams, a belly of concrete, liquid lead flowing through her veins.

'What's your real name?' the boy asked.

She thought for a moment. 'Emilie.'

Bradwen rolled onto his side very easily, leaving his right hand under his cheek and scratching his chest with his left. His eyes glowed in the firelight.

'What was Mrs Evans's first name?'

'I don't know. She was Mrs Evans to me.'

'Did you come here often?'

'I used to. In the old days.'

'Did you know Mr Evans too?'

'No. He died when I was two or three.'

'Do you still smell her?'

'What?'

'Do you still smell Mrs Evans? Here, in the house?'

He lifted his head up from his hand. 'No.'

'I do.' The stream was clearly audible here in the study too. More clearly because the window on the drive side was closer to the water than the window in her bedroom. It sounded different, as if it were a different stream. Or a different house.

'How long?' she said after a lengthy pause. 'How long do you think the smell of the dog will linger at the goose field?'

'Fairly long, I'd guess.'

'Hmm.' The wood on the fire crackled. She felt its warmth on the top of her head. The old days, she thought. What does an expression like that mean when you're twenty? Suddenly a thought entered her mind. 'How could you not have known about the stone circle?'

'I did know about it.'

'You said you didn't.'

'Not at all. I said I "didn't notice it". It was misty that day.'

'And you asked me how to get to the mountain.'

'Not how. I asked if you had a suggestion for the most beautiful way to get there.'

'Are you lying or what?'

'No, I'm not lying. Are you?'

'Yes. Constantly.'

The boy sniggered, his chest shaking.

'Your father wanted to tell me how she met her end.'

'Yeah?'

'But I didn't want to listen.'

'No?'

'I wanted to get rid of him as fast as I could.'

Again, he sniggered.

'I'll listen to *you*,' she said, although she was suddenly finding it almost impossible to keep her eyes open.

The boy got up off the divan with his duvet in his hands. 'Move over a bit.'

She did what he asked, laying her arms alongside her body on top of the covers. He lay down next to her, half under his own duvet, his head at the level of her breasts. There was something submissive about it that reminded her of the night Sam came downstairs and laid his head on her knees.

'I found her,' he said.

'You?'

'Did my father say otherwise?'

She thought about it. 'He acted as if he knew all about it.' She had to dig deep for the English, translating was an effort.

'That's true. I arranged it so he'd find her after me. I owed him that much.'

The boy talked. She had to do her best to follow him, trying not to miss bits or let her mind stray, because it was easy to listen to his words as sounds alone. It was summer – last summer, she presumed – and he'd wanted to see Mrs Evans again, maybe for the last time, she was over ninety after all. He'd come by bike from Bangor, not another cyclist on the road. People here don't ride bikes, even though there's a bike rental place right next to the train station – it's for the tourists, who don't use it either. Up the drive: the grass in the fields was very long, which reminded him of his father who was apparently neglecting his mowing duties. Typical. Sam wasn't with him, he'd left him at home. Replying to her question as to where that was, he said, 'Liverpool.' Was that where he studied? 'Yes, at Hope University. Don't tell my father.' Bangor to here was about fifteen miles, he didn't know if Sam could do that running alongside a bike. And, of course, there was always a chance that his father might be here on any given day, the father he'd stolen the dog from. She could have interrupted him at this point, she was feeling hot from the fire and his talk of summer, but she couldn't summon the energy to open her mouth. He'd seen the geese huddled together near the small wooden shed and hadn't found anyone in the house or under the alders along the stream: she used to sit there sometimes on hot days. He'd leant his bike against the side of the pigsty. The geese gaggled excitedly. He'd walked over to them. They reminded him of a group of people standing around a traffic victim, horny with excitement. He climbed over the fence, the geese scattered and there she was, lying where they'd just been standing. Something had been at her. He didn't know if geese would do that, but imagined it was more likely to have been a fox or a bird of prey of some kind. A kite. Not a *vlieger*, she thought, a *wouw*, and she opened her eyes so that she would see the ceiling of the study and not a goose field in the summer and an old woman lying there dead. He'd only glanced at her. Her dress had been pushed up, he found that worst of all. He ran out of the goose field. A moment before he'd been hungry. On the bike he'd been looking forward to huge pieces of home-made cake. Mrs Evans did that better than anyone, cake-making. He realised that he had to phone someone. He'd grabbed the bike and ridden out to the road. There, at the gate that was always open, he'd rung his father, confident that he wouldn't be home at that time of day. He'd done his best to sound different, leaving a short, deep-voiced message on the answering machine. Then he'd cycled back to Bangor, returned the bike and got on the train. Change at Chester. Final destination: Liverpool Lime Street. The girl in the room next to his at the student house said that the dog had howled all day and asked him to leave it with her next time he planned to go off somewhere alone.

A girl, she thought. 'Will we see your father around here again?' she asked.

'I don't think so. He's got his dog back and you weren't interested.'

Almost unnoticed, the boy had joined her under the duvet. She must have lost the feeling in her left arm for a moment. She didn't complain, this body full of heavy things was not that delicate. He was giving off something, a kind of electricity: his chest shimmered, his hand smouldered, his breath was as hot as a happy dog's. What would it feel like if she weren't wearing her nightie? She wanted to take it off, but the fire had made her sluggish and it was the middle of the night; she was tired, exhausted. 'Can you . . .?' she asked, raising her head slightly off the pillow.

He understood and soon they were lying next to each other in their underpants like two wary adolescents. Her on her back and him on his side, still a little lower, his nose against her upper arm, his arms against her hips. Arms full of tension, she could feel it radiating. The stream was rushing. Just when the sound of the flowing water was about to give way to sleep, he said, 'We're going to the mountain. The day after tomorrow. Christmas Day. The train's running.'

Fine, she thought. To the mountain, I should be able to manage that. 'Will you go to the baker's tomorrow? To buy some Christmas pudding? Give them both my greetings. The fondest greetings from the Dutchwoman.'

The boy made a sound at the back of his throat and fell asleep. Did he find her old and ugly? Could he smell something? She sighed and closed her eyes. Don't think about it. Not now.

55

The boy had gone to the baker's. On foot. She had the house to herself until he came back. Then he had to go to Tesco's to get some food in for Christmas. The radio was on. She was sitting at the kitchen table with the woolly hat on her head. In front of her: Dickinson's *Collected Poems*, open at pages 216 and 217, 'A Country Burial'. She'd written down two translations of the first line and crossed them both out: ~~Spreid ruim dit bed~~ and ~~Spreid dit bed breeduit~~. The first one was a syllable short and the second alliterated where the original didn't. In the end she shifted the meaning slightly and came up with *Spreid dit bed met zorg*, 'Make this bed with care'. The second line was crossed out too: ~~Spreid het met ontzag~~. She'd changed that to *Spreid het ademloos*, 'Make it breathlessly', 'with bated breath'. She'd written the third and fourth lines on a separate sheet that was otherwise covered with individual words: variations on 'judgement', 'excellent' and the several distinct meanings of 'fair'. The rhythm is most important here, she'd thought. She wrote the four lines down again on a third sheet of paper and gazed out of the window. The flowering plants just kept flowering. Dickson's Garden Centre delivered quality. The radio played Christmas evergreen after Christmas evergreen, a calm voice announcing the titles after every third song. She got stuck on the first two lines of the second quatrain. That strange imperative still baffled her, it baffled her completely. 'Be its mattress straight / Be its pillow round'.

The smell of old Mrs Evans grew too strong, she had to go outside. She didn't put on her coat. Not going outside without a coat is for healthy people who are afraid of catching a cold, she thought. She stopped under the rose arch and stared at how the new slate path came to a dead end on the lawn. It wasn't right. It needed something at the end. The path had to lead somewhere, to a pillar maybe, with a big pot on it. The stream murmured, the fallen oak lay dead still. She couldn't imagine the alders ever budding again; there seemed to be no life left in the stumps at all. She went round the side of the house. The geese were tearing at the grass. Still four of them. She wondered if foxes hibernated too. Asleep in a den with a bulging stomach, its snout between its paws, sighing now and then with contentment? She pressed her palms against her temples because she noticed that she was measuring her thoughts in rhythmic syllables, and changed the 'contentment' in her last thought to 'satisfaction'. There was no wind, not a breath of it. The geese saw her and started to cluck softly. She leant on the thick wall. Do they think I'm a goose too, just like the dog thought I was a dog, according to the boy? No, I look more like a turkey, she thought, tugging on the tassels of the purple hat.

A few minutes later she was back at the kitchen table. Instead of returning to what she'd written, she leafed through the section titled NATURE. After a while – she'd almost finished the section – the letters started to run together, making it more and more difficult to read. She didn't find the words 'goose' or 'geese' anywhere. Just as she'd thought. It was all 'bees' and 'butterflies' and 'robins'. She sniffed, clapped the book shut and pushed it away. Dragged herself upstairs, pressed a tablet out of the strip, went back downstairs and poured herself a glass of white wine. Taking the tablet with the wine. When she heard footsteps on the slate, everything was pleasantly fuzzy again.

He'd bring the bread in, then they might talk about the shopping list, then he'd leave again. She would order him to leave. As if he were a dog. He would go to buy superfluous things. Afterwards, possibly after a second tablet, she would get ready. Taking bread and wine to the old pigsty, cushions and rugs, trimming the end of a candle with a sharp knife so it would fit in the neck of an empty bottle, a box of matches next to it. Tonight he could lie next to her, his head lower than hers, his broad thumbs on her breasts. If he dared, at least.

Bradwen came in. He put his rucksack on the table and took off his hat. 'They said hello back,' he said. 'The baker's wife asked when you'd be coming again yourself.'

She shook her head.

'You on the wine?'

'One glass.'

'She's in a reading club. She said it would be nice if you'd join.'

'A reading club?'

'Yes. She even told me the title of the book she's reading now.'

She looked at him. His hair was stuck to his forehead and, as usual, he didn't run his fingers through it. The grey eyes, the squint that made it so hard to see what he was thinking and feeling. He was different, really different, without the dog. It's his own fault, she thought. I sent him away several times. Water suddenly occurred to her. There has to be water too, wine by itself isn't enough. While she was adding it to the shopping list on the kitchen table, she tried to picture the faces of Rhys Jones and his estate agent friend. Not the stony expression of the former, seven or so days ago, or the supposedly jovial look of the latter, a few months ago, but their surprised faces about a week from now. She only half succeeded, she had no recollection of the estate agent's features at all. She tapped a cigarette out of the packet and lit it with a match. Without thinking she drew on it hard and didn't know what hit her: it was so horrible that she didn't take the time to use her fingers but just spat it out. It landed on one of the sheets of paper she had written on. When the boy noticed that she was going to leave it there, he picked it up for her and pressed down on the smouldering paper with one thumb. Then he walked over to the sink and held the cigarette under the tap before throwing it in the bin.

'Did Mrs Evans smoke?' she asked, after she'd taken a mouthful of wine and had to swallow again emphatically to keep down the rising nausea.

'No.' The boy stayed near the sink.

'You have to go and do the shopping.'

'You coming?'

'No. I've got things to do.'

He gestured at the table. 'Were you working?'

'You could just go away for good,' she said.

'How do you mean?'

'I mean what I say.'

'You don't give up, do you?'

She wanted to look straight into his eyes, but couldn't because the window, the light, was behind him. 'Don't say I didn't warn you,' she said.

He stood there with his bum against the sink, then started taking the bread out of his rucksack. 'I miss Sam,' he said. 'That's all.'

She sniffed. Despite the lack of wind, her excursion outdoors had dispelled the old-woman smell, but now it was rising again from her clothes, drifting up from her shoulders. 'Get going,' she said.

He picked up the shopping list. 'Why do I have to buy so much water?' he asked.

'I'm starting to get sick of the tap water,' she said.

'Have you got some money for me?' he asked.

56

The ferry's departure was delayed. There was a problem with one of the propellers. They announced over the PA that divers had been sent down to fix it, without specifying exactly what the problem was. The husband and the policeman drank a second whisky. It was busy on the boat. Fake Christmas trees everywhere, fairy lights, boisterous Brits and quiet Dutchies. Someone was up on a small stage entertaining people. They were sitting off to one side at a round table that was bolted to the floor, next to a window that had rainwater trickling across it on the outside. Through the window they could look out over an enormous expanse of brightly lit petrochemical industry. Somewhere far below them was the policeman's car, among hundreds of other cars. Christmas Eve. Force 5 to 6 winds, north-westerly.

'We won't arrive at nine in the morning then,' the husband said.

'Doesn't matter,' the policeman said. 'We're not in a hurry, are we?'

'No.' He sipped his whisky: the policeman had got both rounds at the bar, which was decorated with lots of brass. 'A fine Scotch,' he'd said, 'single malt.' It tasted smoky, peaty. The policeman knew what he was talking about; the husband hardly ever drank spirits. Now that he was sitting here, he remembered a crossing he'd made long ago with a friend from high school. They drank gin and tonics because they were travelling to England. The friend had spent the whole night puking into the shared toilet in the corridor; he had warded off the nausea by rubbing his breastbone for hours, lying motionless on his back on a narrow bed in a windowless cabin with two complete strangers in the next bunk. That was before he knew his wife. Now he knew her and now he was drinking whisky, a drink for grown men, he thought, but equally good, or even better, as a way of getting in the mood for England. Packed in his travel bag, dozens of metres lower in the boat, was a marble cake his mother-in-law had made. That was a tradition: when they went on holiday, she produced a marble cake for them to eat at their destination, whether it was a campsite or a hotel room. As if this were an ordinary holiday, as if she hadn't noticed that her son-in-law was going away with the policeman, not her daughter. He looked at the man on the chair next to him. He had just taken a sip of whisky and was watching the entertainer put a hat on a redhead he'd hauled up onto the stage; he let the whisky wash around his mouth before swallowing it. Even out of uniform he looked like a policeman. Maybe because he knew what he looked like *in* uniform.

'I'm not looking forward to it,' he said.

'The wind's not that strong,' the policeman said.

'No, not the crossing.'

'Oh, that.'

'Yes, *that*. I wish it was just a normal trip.'

'Imagine it is.' The policeman drank his whisky, seemingly at ease.

The husband looked at the stage, where a clown had now appeared. The large room smelt of chips and deep-fried snacks. 'I'm going to go and lie down,' he said.

'Fine,' said the policeman.

The cabin was nothing like the cramped closet next to the engine room he remembered from more than twenty years ago. Two beds with a picture above each bed and a large window between them, a small hallway with a wardrobe and a toilet with a sink. The husband sat on one of the beds and poked a knitting needle in under his cast. The policeman got undressed, folding his clothes neatly before laying them on a small bench. He went into the toilet. In the cabin you could feel the ship hum and shudder. It was as if it wanted to leave but was being held back. The dark cold sea. Scratching with the knitting needle gave him virtually no relief. He heard the policeman clear his throat and spit, then turn on the tap. A little later he flushed the toilet. Anton was his name.

Hours later the husband woke up. The ship was on its way, rising and falling. Somewhere in the depths, a car alarm howled constantly. With every movement – up and down, side to side – he tensed his muscles, pushing back as if to stop the ship from capsizing. Had his school friend convinced him that you could hold back nausea by rubbing your breastbone? The ceiling light was still glowing: after being turned off, it had switched to a kind of emergency setting.

The policeman was asleep, breathing evenly, one hand on his bare chest. There was a completeness about him, everything as it should be. The way he did things, the way he looked. His cropped black hair. The husband couldn't wait to get off the ship. He hoped that it was almost morning and that they would soon be docking in Hull, but he knew they might have just left Rotterdam. He didn't look at his mobile, which was lying on the shelf next to his bed as an alarm clock. He rubbed his breastbone and breathed deeply in and out. It was incredible how lonely it was in the cabin with that weak but inescapable light, a sleeping person next to him, coats on the coat rack swinging away from the wall and flopping back against it to a regular beat. He could get up. The bar might still be open; maybe the clown was still onstage. He imagined the journey his card had made, probably by air. 'I'm coming.' And then? he thought. When it started to get light, he couldn't see anything except grey water through the window.

The ferry arrived in Hull four hours late. The morning had been strange, passengers weren't meant to stay on the boat this long. Staff were few and far between, there was no entertainment, the gambling area was deserted. This boat wasn't set up for meals: it left at 9 p.m. and docked at nine the next morning. The husband and the policeman couldn't find any breakfast. Everywhere people were sitting or walking around with their bags or rucksacks; all they could do was wait.

After driving off the ferry without any hitches, the policeman switched to the left side of the road almost automatically and a navigation system started giving him directions in Dutch. The voice was called Bram. The policeman had the kind of car the husband found slightly annoying when he saw them in Amsterdam. Big and black. He looked around. It was a grey day and Hull was hideous: a broad stretch of water on his left and not a hill in sight. He was exhausted and his itchy leg was driving him to distraction. He hadn't thought to get the knitting needle out of his bag; he might even have left it on the boat. 'Thanks, Bram, we've got the idea,' the policeman said after the voice gave instruction after instruction through a series of roundabouts.

'Can we get a coffee somewhere?' the husband said.

'I'm dying for one too,' the policeman said. 'And something to eat.'

Shortly afterwards there was a sign for a Little Chef. The policeman parked the car and helped the husband out, handing him his crutches. The husband followed him in, stood behind him at the cashpoint, the self-service counter and the checkout, and paid for both of them, joining the policeman at a table by the window, where he watched him eat a chicken roll. For himself he'd taken a bacon-and-egg roll and a large coffee. They ate and drank in silence. When they'd finished, a woman in a red Santa hat cleared away their empty mugs and plates.

'Did you enjoy your meal, guys?' she asked. The policeman told her that it was very tasty, the husband nodded and swallowed the last mouthful. 'Have a wonderful Christmas,' she said and moved on to the next table to clear away their dishes, asking them the same question and wishing them a wonderful Christmas.

'I have to go to the toilet,' the husband said.

'Me too,' said the policeman.

They stood next to each other at the urinals. There was no one else there. Christmas carols were being piped in through hidden speakers.

'Could you call me Anton sometime?' the policeman asked.

'Sure,' said the husband. One of the crutches, leaning against the tiled wall next to the urinal, slid away to one side. He made a grab to catch it, letting go of his penis in the process, which immediately interrupted the flow of urine.

The policeman already had it in his left hand. He kept pissing very calmly. 'Anton,' he said. 'That's my name.' He put the crutch back against the wall, shook his penis dry, put it back in his pants and zipped up.

When the husband washed his hands, he saw a wet spot on his trousers in the mirror.

Before getting back into the car, one of them standing either side, the policeman looked at his watch. 'It's almost three,' he said. 'We – No, it's almost two. But still, it'll be long dark by the time we get there.' The roof of the car came up to his throat.

'Uh-huh?' said the husband. He wanted to get in and stretch the leg with the cast, which was possible if he slid the seat as far back as it went. He wanted to close his eyes and listen to Bram, who would accurately inform them that they needed to cross the next roundabout, second exit. He had a Lucy in his car, a voice with a Flemish accent, who regularly warned him that he needed to make a U-turn, which was, of course, down to his driving style. Bram sounded more confident.

'Should we get a hotel?'

'Yes,' said the husband.

'One day's not going to make any difference, is it?'

'No,' said the husband.

'You OK?' asked the policeman.

'I don't know what to do when we get there.'

'Do you need to know? You'll see what happens.'

'Yes,' said the husband.

'We could just head north,' the policeman said. 'Scotland's closer.'

'No.'

'We could put it off a little. If you'd rather.'

'No.'

'Let's go then. We'll stop when we feel like it.'

The husband laid a hand on the roof of the car. 'Maybe it would have been different if we'd had kids.'

'No. Kids are a pain in the neck.'

'Says you.'

'Yes, says me. Everything should be its own justification.' The policeman opened the door and climbed in behind the wheel.

The husband now had a clear view of the little white man with the cook's hat on the red background. Behind the logo, the sky was an even grey. A flag on the roof of the roadside restaurant hung limply against the pole. The policeman had already started the car. He pulled the door open and sat down, putting his cast in a good position and resting his other leg next to it. He looked past the policeman's shoulder at his hands, which turned the wheel, let it go for a moment, then took it again. Bram told them to turn left, back onto the A63. *Goole* said the signs and *Castleford* and *Leeds*.

A couple of hours later, past Manchester, a large sign on the motorway verge announced *Holiday Inn Runcorn*. It was dark and very busy on the road. 'That's enough for today,' the policeman said. 'Time to eat and drink.'

The husband looked at the hands on the wheel, a silver ring on the thumb of the right hand. The headlights swept over the row of squat conifers that lined the car park.

'Try to make a U-turn,' said Bram.

The policeman laughed.

57

Early in the morning she turned on the TV. A detailed weather forecast showed the map of the UK. It was cloudy almost everywhere except North Wales, and when the clouds started moving it turned out they wouldn't set in here until night, from the west. The temperature was mild for the time of year and the weatherman wished her a 'Merry green Christmas'. She switched it off and went into the kitchen to make some sandwiches. She put four bananas in her rucksack and two plastic water bottles and the sandwiches in the boy's. She looked at the packet of cigarettes in the middle of the table, hesitated, then put it in her bag too. She pulled on her boots and stuck her head out the front door to see if the alder branch was still leaning against the wall. She mustn't forget it. Stars were still visible in the sky, already paling. She pulled on the purple hat. 'Come on!' she called from the bottom of the stairs.

The boy had dared to stroke her breasts, although she'd needed to encourage him. Shivering, she'd lain on her back. His hot breath on her throat, the warmth of the fire, not on the top of her head, but on the side of her body. He'd turned the mattress ninety degrees; he must have done it sometime that day. He'd laid the portrait of Dickinson face down on the table. They'd hardly seen each other all day: him gone, her back and forth to the pigsty; him back, her in front of the TV; him in the kitchen preparing yet more food to feed his wiry lamb's body, her in the claw-foot bath with Native Herbs to banish the old-woman smell. 'You moved her out of the way and turned her upside down,' she'd said, after turning onto her side. 'Yes,' he'd replied, his lips very close to hers, carefully blowing his breath into her mouth. 'Spooky woman.' He can suck it out of me, she'd thought. Maybe he can banish it. 'Don't we need to . . .?' he'd said, his lamb's body over hers, his fists next to her upper arms, a tendon that ran straight across his chest trembling. She'd stroked his bum without answering, looking past his chest to his eager penis and very slowly pulling him down. Protection, she'd thought, that's for healthy people. It was unbelievable how warm he was. Warm and young and alive. As usual, she hadn't been able to choose – looking straight into both eyes wasn't possible – but she'd kept looking, hoping that he would go slowly, that she wouldn't need to say anything, that his lamb's body would feel hers and merge with it. She was staring intently at the very instant that the eye with the squint pulled a little to one side and she was able, very briefly, to look him straight in both eyes after all, even though he'd probably not seen a thing for those few seconds. She'd sighed deeply; he hadn't made a sound and wanted to get off her almost immediately. 'No,' she'd said and hugged him tight, his wet chest against her breasts. With the spread fingers of her left hand, she'd finally combed the hair over his forehead. The boy had licked her neck. Without getting sick. Later he'd gone back to his divan, after setting the last logs on the fire. He'd done that very quietly, not a single joint in his wiry body had creaked. She had lain on her side, staring at the fire. She could smell herself and she could smell the boy: the smell from the beginning, the combination of sweet socks and bitter leaves. He had snored slightly, it was more a quiet whistling. She had wanted to fall asleep in that moment, preferably together with him, doing at least one thing together, but instead the old-woman smell rose again from the bed or the floor or her own body. She cried quietly and thought that she should stop resisting. And finally, with the stream rushing the whole time, she imagined the house, the geese and the sheep, the alders and the gorse bushes, the reservoir, the stone circle and the rose garden, her own small world, and fell asleep.

The boy hadn't sucked anything out of her, he hadn't banished it. She could feel her body, there was very little energy in it. The train went slowly, thick clouds of steam and smoke – white and black – passed the windows. A conductor with an old-fashioned ticket machine hung around his bulging stomach came to punch their tickets and there was even an old man pushing a refreshment cart down the aisle. Volunteers. The boy took a coffee and a piece of fruit cake. When she saw that he wasn't reaching for his wallet, she paid. He was no different to any other day, at most slightly excited at the prospect of climbing a mountain. They were sitting in padded seats with armrests and not, as she had imagined, on wooden benches. It was a Pullman carriage, first class, painted reddish brown. She had paid for the tickets. The boy had driven to Caernarfon. They were sitting opposite each other. Sitting next to each other was impossible in this carriage: she was facing forward; Bradwen, back. A cream-coloured curtain was swinging to and fro next to her head. Outside were green and brown fields, stone walls everywhere, bare trees with grey trunks, hills on their left that kept growing.

'Not much snow,' the boy said, with his mouth full of fruit cake and his face pressed against the window. 'Maybe at the top. We have to get off in a minute.'

She didn't say anything. She would say very little all day. Her suspicions had been aroused.

Rhyd Ddu station consisted of a single platform with a wooden waiting room and two rectangular beds of rocks and plants. There were a couple of houses in the distance. She got off the train and almost had to hold her breath, it smelt that fresh here. Fresh and sharp; she had no idea what she was smelling. Dead ferns? Rocks and boulders?

Water? Pure air? A few other people had got off too. She looked up past a gently sloping hill. 'Come on,' said the boy. She gripped the alder branch tightly and followed. The sun shone in her face through the small panes in the waiting room, which together formed one large window. Like an ambitious film extra, a railway guard held a signalling disc aloft. The train moved off, blowing out clouds of black smoke.

A wide path which was raised in the middle led up past a shed that reminded her of the old pigsty. The boy walked ahead without looking back, but she didn't want to ask him to slow down already. She concentrated on her stick and her breathing. Now and then she looked ahead or around. Sheep country without sheep, a neglected stone wall, wire fences, hikers. Looking back, she realised that she and the boy were bringing up the rear. The tractor path wound its way up slowly; she breathed in and out evenly, adjusting the swinging of the stick to the rhythm of her breathing. Why didn't the boy look back at her even once? Look, she thought. Smell, feel. The sun is shining.

'Wait!' she called.

The boy waited until she was just behind him, then walked on. It was still fairly easy, you couldn't call it a steep climb. In the far distance, a good bit higher, probably at the top, there was some kind of structure. The summit was completely white.

'See that bump a bit to the right?' the boy asked.

She looked along his outstretched arm. 'Yes.'

'We're going to walk around that now. And see that ridge to the left of it that looks like it's lower than the bump?'

'Yes.'

'That's the crest we take to the summit.'

'How far is that from here?'

'It looks further than it is.'

'Oh.'

'Yr Wyddfa is the name of the mountain. Burial place.'

She looked at her feet. The path, the small stones, the short flattened grass. She wasn't dizzy but her field of vision seemed unsteady, pivoting around the fixed point of her shoes and the end of her stick. Today, after taking two tablets, the pain was distant. She had actually had surprisingly little pain, it was more a vague but persistent sense of deterioration, a shrinking of her body, her mouth spouting words that weren't in her head. Maybe she hadn't had any pain because she had been on painkillers almost constantly. The boy had just said something incomprehensible, she only understood what he was talking about because she could see the cover of the Ordnance Survey map before her: *Snowdon / Yr Wyddfa*. She didn't care what the name meant. As far as she was concerned the boy was already gone, he could say what he liked, he wouldn't get much more out of her than 'Oh', 'Yes' or 'No'. Maybe he'd fall off the mountain. She took a deep breath, the bite was gone from the air. The path, his heels, the grass. Walk. Keep walking. The path curved to the right and went through a brand-new gate and suddenly they were at the top of a cliff. An enormous void on her left, a couple of small lakes far below. Maybe *I'll* fall off the mountain, she thought. Her head was itchy under the hat, the tassels swung back and forth annoyingly. She was trying with all her might to make it a day like any other and the swishing purple tassels helped, as did the clear path. The sun that cast a red and blue glow over the lakes. Red and blue. They looked minuscule from up here. Not much bigger than, say, a hotel pond. They were probably deeper. She thought of the bananas in her rucksack or were they in Bradwen's? He had the water, she was sure of that. Maybe tomorrow would be a day like any other too, she hadn't decided yet.

'I'm thirsty,' she said.

The boy stopped and took off his rucksack. He got out a bottle of water and handed it to her. She drank, water ran down her chin. Quickly she handed the bottle back. He drank too, but only after sticking a thumb in the neck and rotating it, his index finger squeezed against the thread. No, in the train just now he hadn't been acting as if nothing had happened. 'Onwards,' she said.

Did the Evanses ever climb this mountain? They must have. Or was a mountain here like the Stedelijk Museum in Amsterdam for her? So close you took it for granted and never went. She imagined the boy as Farmer Evans on a sunny Sunday in his younger years and herself as his new bride, a girl with no interest at all in the cliff, the lakes or black birds, who can't take her eyes off her husband's back, longing for children. 'Hey,' she called. 'Did Mrs Evans have children?'

'No,' said the boy, who was already a good ten metres ahead. He turned back, then walked on. 'Otherwise they'd be living in your house now. Or sold it, at least.'

All at once she was exhausted and widowed, with the

old-woman smell forcing its way into her nostrils. The boy was leaving her farther and farther behind. Her bones creaked, her corns were playing up, the wind tugged a lock of thin grey hair out of her bun. But I already knew that, she thought. Rhys Jones told me. Rhys Jones, his father. Why is the boy so keen to get away from me? She looked slightly to the left, following the ridge to the top. It seemed very far away. It was terribly white up there. The structure could just be an enormous pile of snow. I'll never make it, she thought. Suddenly one of her legs was dragging.

Her aunt cheering her uncle on like a fanatical football supporter. She has something in her hand, an object. Her uncle working faster and faster: sawing, varnishing, hammering. Cats fleeing under the sofa. 'Not a wall unit,' she says. 'Not a wall unit.' Her aunt laughs, still cheering him on, urging him forward. Her mother's there too. *That's how you do it! You just do things!* One of the cats, the oldest, a tortoiseshell, slinks out of the house.

'Wall unit?'

She opened her eyes. The boy was very close to her.

'What?'

'You said something about a wall unit.'

'Not at all.' Slowly she raised herself. Bright sunlight. Her shoulder touched something, a remnant of a wall. She used her arms to push herself farther up and leant on the sharp stones, the rucksack an awkward hunch between her back and the wall. They'd been climbing constantly and now she saw the depths for the first time: a model train station, an enormous lake beside the tracks, other mountains, hills, hazy sunlight – the picture on a box for a homeopathic cure. She panted. The boy squatted before her and pulled her a little closer by the shoulders. Then he wormed the rucksack off her back and got out the bunch of bananas. He gave her one and ate two himself, putting the skins in his own bag.

'I'm going on,' he said. 'I'll be back before you know it.'

'Cat,' she said.

'What?'

'Cat.' I can, she thought, that's what I want to say. Not *cat*, but *can*, with something else. I *can* walk to the top, if we don't go too fast. Something like that.

'Just wait here,' he said. 'Really. I'll be back soon.' He turned and walked off.

She watched him go. He strode up the slope like a mountain sheep, reaching the line where the grass gave way to snow. She turned back to the view and peeled the banana, stuffing it into her mouth and throwing the skin over her shoulder. 'I'm fine,' she said to a couple of concerned hikers. 'Just enjoying the view.' That last bit was a mistake because the man and woman turned and began to provide a commentary on all they could see. They were in her way, they were mosquitoes, annoying blowflies.

'What a lovely knitted cap you have,' the woman said before they finally walked on. She pulled the strip of tablets out of the front pocket of the rucksack and took one with a couple of mouthfuls of icy water. She breathed in and out deeply and rubbed her legs, then rummaged through the front pocket again for the packet of cigarettes and a box of matches. She sat with her hands on her lap, then lit a match.

It kept burning, there was virtually no wind. She braced herself. The tar and nicotine that assaulted her throat were almost liquid. She had just enough time to hurl the cigarette as far away as possible before bending over to one side and vomiting up the banana. She sat up straight, breathed in and out again deeply and looked at the thin plume of smoke. She drank a few mouthfuls of the sweet-tasting water, spitting out the last one, then stood up and started to walk downhill. She didn't look at the drop or the model train station, but at the path, her shoes, the alder branch and the purple tassels waltzing around her head.

Later – she didn't know how much later – the boy walked up onto the platform. She was sitting on the ground, leaning against the wall of the waiting room. The door was locked. A group of hikers was standing a bit farther along. Every now and then they had looked at her. For a long time she'd stared at a construction next to the tracks: a red tank on very tall black legs, with a spout. She got up to her feet. When the boy was standing in front of her – he had warm cheeks and was giving off the metallic smell of thin mountain air, the only thing missing was for him to let his tongue loll out of his mouth like a happy dog's – she asked, 'What do you see?'

It took him a second to answer. 'A woman with a very nice purple beanie. She's tired. She didn't make it to the top, but that's not the end of the world. It's Christmas, and time she went home. There is cooking and drinking to be done.'

58

Bradwen turned into the drive and stopped. He pointed at the letter box. 'Have you ever looked in there?'

'No.'

'Shall I?'

'No.'

He drove on.

She saw sheep in the field along the road. 'Stop,' she said. The boy braked.

'I do want to.'

'Shall I drive back?'

'No, I'll walk.' She pushed the car door open. It was very heavy. A few sheep looked up, but most kept grazing the grass that was new to them. She lifted the lid of the letter box. There was very little in there. Had they given up on advertising here? Or did the postman know that Mrs Evans was no longer reading her letters? When she picked up a couple of brochures, an envelope slid out from between them, landing with a clunk on the bottom of the letter box. She put the brochures back and pulled it out. Her name and the name of the house. *Gwynedd*. Was that the county? The postmark was clearly legible. She tore open the envelope and pulled out a card. 'I'm coming,' it said, with her name and her husband's. She turned the card over and stared at the dog on the front. It was a puppy in a basket. She

looked south, at the mountain. Yes, it looked very easy . . .
From here.

'Anything in there?' the boy asked.

'No,' she said. 'Rubbish. Advertising.'

I moved the sheep (not that it is of any concern to you).
Williams and Goodwin, Estate Agents, Valuers, Surveyors
and Auctioneers, and I will come round on the 1st of January.
Be sure to have enough cash for the lost geese. Stuck to the
window of the front door with a piece of chewing gum.

'Does that man smell it when we're away?' she said.

The boy didn't answer, he sniffed.

She leant the alder branch against the wall and went
inside. The kitchen clock said quarter to four. The Christmas-
tree lights were on. Bradwen walked over to the stove, put
in a few logs and started to stoke the fire. She stood in the
kitchen looking at his back. The wiry lamb's body, ready to
leap. She had to restrain herself from rummaging through
the sideboard straight away in search of things that would
be useful. First things first, she thought.

'You've done something to the sofa,' the boy said. 'It's
like it's bigger.'

She didn't say anything.

He walked to the fridge and got out the open bottle of white
wine. He hadn't yet taken off his coat. He still had his hat on.

Now, she thought. But how? 'Wait,' she said.

'What for?'

'Come with me.' She walked ahead to the front door.

'What are we going to do?'

'Come.' She crossed the slate path to the old pigsty. She

heard him following her. There was an orange glow over the goose field, the pigsty wall on the garden side was already in shadow. She pulled open the door and flicked on the light. 'There,' she said, pointing to the concrete steps.

'What's down there?'

'Go and look. At the back.'

'Have you got another Christmas present for me?'

'Not so many questions. Just look.' She stepped aside. The boy went down the steps, bending, one hand on the edge of the opening. 'It's dark,' he said. He looked up at her. Like a dog, she thought. Like Sam after he's been given an order he doesn't entirely trust.

She turned her head away, looking for the wooden slat she'd used weeks before to measure the rectangle on the lawn.

'You'll get used to it in a minute.'

She saw his blue hat disappear, then pulled on the top of the trapdoor, slamming it shut. It bounced a couple of times. She stood on the trapdoor and, taking the wooden slat, got down on her knees to slide it through the two brackets on either side. Then she braced herself, waiting for the pounding and the yelling. Nothing. The boy kept quiet: maybe he thought she was playing a game. She stood up as carefully as she could, as if sound from her would evoke sound from him. She took a step back through the open door. Another step. She was outside. It's over in no time, she thought. A lot sooner than I thought. She left the light on: maybe it would be of some use to him, through the cracks and the chinks. She might switch it off later. She turned and walked back to the house.

*

She poured herself a glass of wine and took her time over the first mouthful. The radio had to be on, but not on a station playing Christmas evergreens. She adjusted the frequency until she heard classical music. Then she went down on her knees a second time and started to go through the contents of the sideboard. Soon after, she started on the big job of moving the mattress, duvets, bin bags, an old-fashioned lamp she could put a candle in and a bottle of water. The wheelbarrow had been a good buy: once she had it balanced, she could even wheel the mattress. It seemed dark, but the time it took her to reach the goose field was enough for her to realise that there was still some light, even if the orange glow was gone. Somewhere behind her the geese clucked excitedly as she prepared it all, working stubbornly, without thinking. She had brought pliers to remove a plank and bend back the chicken wire, but spreading the bin bags was unexpectedly difficult and her hands and knees were soon filthy. She was sweating and breathing heavily. During the short walk from the gate back to the house, she felt like the empty wheelbarrow was the only thing keeping her upright. The gate had been open for quite a while and still the stupid birds hadn't fled. She tiptoed over to the pigsty and turned off the light. No sound from downstairs. She left the door open.

It was still classical music. She was no expert and never recognised anything, but classical music seemed to have more eternal value than Christmas evergreens. She turned it up a little. It was quarter to eight. The Ordnance Survey map lay spread out on the kitchen table. *Snowdon / Yr Wyddfa*. Now and then she looked at the dotted green lines, screwing up her eyes to make them blur and come together on her land and, if possible, in the goose field. Her husband's postcard was lying on the map with the written side up. Dickinson lay next to it as if it had to be there, open. In the living room, the fire in the stove was slowly dying. Even if she'd wanted to add some fresh wood, she couldn't; the pile was gone. She ate two more bananas, which she kept down. An empty stomach wasn't a good idea, she guessed. Now and then she got up to pace between the table and the sink or the sideboard, on which she'd stood a torch she'd dug out of a drawer that had also contained new batteries. Slowly, in half-glasses, she drank the white wine until the bottle was almost empty. Chardonnay. Alcohol. She suspected that would help. The boy had bought it. She didn't have the slightest inclination to turn on the TV. At eight o'clock she went upstairs.

The water was on the verge of being too hot. And clear. No Native Herbs tonight. She'd opened the bathroom window. If she didn't splash too loudly she could hear the stream flowing. She stared at the scar on her foot. It had healed beautifully. Despite the open window, the mirror was already steaming over. She was glad of that. She tried to relax, but kept listening carefully. The *I'm coming* on the postcard was disquieting. Rhys Jones's *Be sure* was an imperative and had nothing in common with *Be its mattress straight*. She closed her eyes. Bees, clover, white roses, a woman making a bed, shaking out a bottom sheet so that it spreads wide and descends over a firm mattress, a crisp pillowcase on a feather pillow. *Ample make this bed*. She opened her eyes, staring at the ceiling light. Subjunctive mood. It was a subjunctive. Just as Dickinson didn't write *Make this bed ample*, she didn't write *Its mattress be straight / Its pillow be round*. Hold on. Don't think. Stay lying here until my whole body is hot through and through and it will take a long time for me to get cold again. So hot, I'll wish I was cold. Twenty minutes later she pulled on clean clothes: trousers, blouse, baggy jumper. White sports socks. She went downstairs. In the kitchen, a final half-glass of wine. A sheet of paper, a brown felt tip. For a second, she saw the boy drawing circles with it. It was a sheet of paper that should have been used to plan a garden. In a few minutes she was finished – shaking her head, true, because she couldn't believe it had taken her so long to see something so obvious. It was quarter to nine. She unplugged the radio and flicked the switch to battery. The music only missed a couple of beats. She didn't unplug the Christmas-tree lights and left the lights on in the kitchen, living room, bathroom and study. She put on the purple hat. She left the front door unlocked.

She walked down the drive to the goose field, lighting her way with the torch. No stars: it was overcast, as predicted. There was a very slight drizzle. Climbing over the gate was draining; she leant back against the boards for a moment and searched for the geese with the narrow beam. The birds evaded her of course. She picked up the radio and walked to the goose shelter, where she took off her boots on the bin bag lying in front of the entrance. Radio inside, where it sounded louder. Outside it had also had to compete with the plaintive cry of an owl. Or a kite. She struck a match and lit the candle in the lantern. She wasn't cold; the hot bath had done its job well. She tried to pull the piece of chicken wire back over the entrance and finished by taking the bin bag that was lying outside and folding it up. She'd brought the entire supply of tablets. It would take at least twenty; that was her estimate. More would probably be better, though maybe not. She swallowed them one at a time, sitting up and washing each one down with a mouthful of water from the plastic bottle she'd put there earlier. Then she lay down under the two duvets, taking deep breaths. The light from the lantern wasn't flickering, the ceiling of the shelter was evenly lit. She thought of the fox – *a* fox really, she'd never seen it – and of the badger and grey squirrels. All hibernating. This too was a kind of den in which to hibernate. A gentle light, the muffled rushing of the stream and the dull tap of the odd raindrop. Even now, having lain in the bath for so long and putting on clean clothes, she could still smell old Mrs Evans. She couldn't help but smile. It didn't matter, it didn't matter at all. She closed her eyes and opened them again when she felt a strange pressure against her feet. One of the geese was on the mattress, the other three were sitting close by. All four deeply calm, but not sleeping. That's a shame, she was still able to think. Not having any bread with me. The goose that was on the mattress lowered its head until it was resting on her legs. It felt like a rope, a cord pulling her away. I've turned into a goose, she thought. Away from here, through the rickety tarred roof. Over the field, feet first into the sky, between the branches and the electricity lines. *Let no sunrise' yellow noise / Interrupt this ground*. With any luck, all the way to the top of the mountain.

59

'Impervious,' the husband said. 'That's the word.'

'You're not exactly an open book yourself,' the policeman said.

They were eating an English breakfast, announced on the counter as a Boxing Day Breakfast. The husband was drinking a glass of champagne. Very disgusting, pink champagne. 'Be grateful you're driving,' he said to the policeman. They were eating sausages, grilled tomatoes, bacon, fried eggs and beans.

'Not open?' the husband said. 'What do you mean by that?'

'Just that you're hard to figure out, for me.'

'I suppose you think I find you easy?' He pushed the glass aside. 'Anton.'

The policeman didn't have an answer to that. He put a last piece of sausage in his mouth and looked at his watch. After breakfast they went upstairs and packed their bags. The husband paid for the room, which was a lot more expensive than he'd expected.

A very light rain was falling. 'Then we're both impervious,' the husband said as they got into the big black car. Walking felt easier this morning. He counted back through the weeks and realised it was almost time to have the cast taken off.

'That's got you thinking, hasn't it?' the policeman said.

'Yep.'

The policeman drove out of the car park like a boy racer, swinging the wheel and wrenching the gearstick.

The husband positioned his cast and looked out. When he burped, he tasted the disgusting champagne. He didn't think ahead. Even doing his best, he found it difficult to picture his wife's face. *I'm coming.* It was really only because he knew she was ill. Otherwise he would probably have stayed away.

'This friend of yours,' he said.

'No,' said the policeman.

'No?'

'Don't talk about it. We're abroad.'

'Do you even have a friend?'

Bram interrupted, telling them to cross the next roundabout. Second exit. *Hapsford, Ellesmere Port.* On the roundabout Bram continued to give them directions.

The husband watched the policeman's hands, relaxed on the steering wheel. The windscreen wipers had stopped slapping back and forth. There was a break in the clouds ahead. 'It's going to be a nice day,' he said.

'Yes,' said the policeman.

'There is a chance, of course, that's she no longer there.'

'We'll see when we get there.'

'"Boxing Day", what's that actually mean?'

'I don't know.'

In eight hundred metres, bear right. Then take the motorway. The husband was starting to get fed up with Bram. He couldn't be bothered trying to talk over him. He closed his eyes and thought about running. With a foot that wasn't broken, that rolled. Running, breathing, sweating, clenching his fists to squeeze the pain out of his spleen. Coming home alone, showering, stretching out on the sofa. She never said anything. In all those years she hadn't once asked how it had gone. Sometimes she sighed. She'd never put in an appearance at a race either. Impervious. He thought of something his mother-in-law had said. *It's still all your fault.* Because he, as the policeman said, was hardly an open book himself? His foot wasn't itchy; he didn't miss the knitting needle. That was probably a sign that things were going well under the plaster.

Northop, Brynford, Rhuallt. Bram hadn't said a word for ages, presumably because they were on the A55 and would be staying on it for a while. The sun was now shining; the fields and woods were steaming. It's beautiful here, the husband thought. His phone started to vibrate against his chest. He pulled it out of the breast pocket of his coat.

'You there yet?' His mother-in-law.

'No.'

'Why not?'

'The boat was delayed. We had to spend a night in a hotel.'

'But now you're almost there?'

'About another hour and a half, I think.'

'What's the weather like?'

'Nice. The sun's shining.'

'It's terrible here. Not cosy at all.'

The husband glanced to one side. The policeman was looking ahead imperturbably. 'Well, it's very cosy here. I drank champagne this morning.'

'What? Why for God's sake?'

'It's Boxing Day.'

'What's that?'

'I don't know. The second day of Christmas?'

'Does that policeman of yours know how to get there?'

'He's got help. From Bram.'

'Bram?'

'One of those navigation systems.'

'Oh.' There was a moment's silence. 'Is he wearing his uniform?'

'No, why should he? He's not working.'

'No, I thought, because he's kind of going there to pick her up in an official capacity.'

'This has nothing to do with the police.'

'That's true.' There was another silence in Amsterdam. 'Your father-in-law wants to know if they showed a film on the boat.'

'Not that I know of. But it was a very big boat. We saw a clown on a stage.'

'Look, when you're there, will you tell her that we . . .'

'Yes?'

They consulted again. 'Well, that we love her. And that we want her to come home. Not to us, of course, but to you.'

'To me? I thought it was all my fault.'

'No. According to your father-in-law, that's not right. We talked about it some more.'

'Oh.'

'We love her, her father too. Tell her that. Will you do that?'

'Of course I'll tell her. When we get there, I'll give her my phone, then you can tell her yourself.'

'No, you do it. And then we'll call afterwards. Or no, you call us, because we won't know when you get there. What time is it there anyway?'

'An hour earlier than with you.'

'OK, we don't want to be in the middle of dinner.'

The man shook his head.

'You can also tell her that it's not on, just disappearing like that. That she should think of her old mum and dad. And that we've forgiven her.'

'What have you forgiven her?'

'You know, that thing with the, um . . . Everybody does things they end up regretting.' His father-in-law said something in the background. 'Your father-in-law says, "The flesh is weak."' She started to cry.

The husband moved the phone away from his ear. 'I've got my mother-in-law on the line,' he told the policeman. 'She says the flesh is weak.'

The policeman glanced at him. 'Can't argue with that,' he said.

'Something else.' Now he heard his father-in-law's voice. He pressed the phone against his ear again. 'Tell her that we really want to celebrate New Year together, all of us.'

'I'll do that. Are you going to come here or do you mean in Amsterdam?'

'Here, of course! What would we want to go there for? Do you really see me getting your mother-in-law on one of those boats?'

'You could fly.'

'Not if you paid us. No, here. At our place. In her old home. It'll be good for her. We have to look after her.'

'Yes.'

'You've got a return, haven't you? When are you taking the boat back?'

'No, no return. We can come back whenever we like. Plus we'll have two cars then.'

'You know what? Tell her her uncle and auntie are coming too.' His mother-in-law said something. 'What? Hang on a sec . . . No, of course he won't mind. He's worried about her . . . Why? . . . I guarantee he won't play up . . . Sorry, your mother-in-law said something. I'll arrange it right away. I'm sure she'll enjoy it.'

'I'll let her know.'

More consultations in the background. 'What? Hang on a sec. Your mother-in-law wants to know if the marble cake's OK.'

'It's still in the bag. That's for later.'

'Will you ring up the minute you get there?'

'I promise.'

'OK. Drive safely for the rest of the trip.'

The man put his mobile back in his breast pocket. His ear was hot. 'Shouldn't you call home?' he asked the policeman. 'Just to touch base?'

'No need.'

The A55 was now following the coast. *Colwyn Bay, Llandudno, Conwy.* A train that appeared to run along the beach overtook them.

'Just under an hour,' the policeman said.

'I think it's beautiful here,' the husband said. 'And I wonder what she's been doing all this time.'

'Maybe she's living with a Welsh farmer.'

The husband laughed. They drove through a village where the train was stopped at a station. Land was visible in the distance. The husband wondered if it could be Ireland. A little later the train passed the car again. 'She's a city girl. She can't tell a blackbird from a sparrow.'

'Is that a requirement? You don't need to know stuff like that to live in the country.'

'It's so lonely.'

'And living with you in one house in the city wasn't?'

'What's that supposed to mean?'

The policeman took one hand off the wheel and laid it on the husband's leg.

He didn't move it away because the policeman was the driver.

Turn left ahead. In eight hundred metres, turn left and follow the road. After a long silence Bram had spoken again. *Caernarfon*, the signs said, nine more miles. *At the roundabout, turn right, third exit.* 'Bram's got his work cut out for him now,' the policeman said.

'Can he find a house just by the name?' the husband asked. He rubbed his left knee.

'No.'

'So how are we going to get there?'

The policeman took a map from the pocket in his door and gave it to the husband, saying, 'What would you do without me?'

The husband looked at the map. *Snowdon / Yr Wyddfa, Explorer Map.* A mountaineer in a bright red coat standing on a rock with a snow-covered mountaintop in the background.

'I drew a circle around the house,' the policeman said. 'And used yellow highlighter on the road to get there.'

The husband tried to unfold the map but couldn't, it was much too big. Too big and too detailed and it also made an incredible racket. He laid the map on his lap. The land across the water on their right was a lot closer; it couldn't possibly be Ireland. *Take the exit. Keep left, then cross the roundabout, second exit.* They drove through the town of Caernarfon. The shops were open and the streets were fairly busy; the husband saw a large sign reading *Sale!* He saw what he thought was a kind of palm tree in the middle of a small roundabout. *Cross the roundabout, second exit.* The husband kept quiet, he couldn't compete with Bram. Was Boxing Day a public holiday when shops held sales?

A quarter of an hour later they stopped at a T-junction. Bram had said, *You have reached your destination*, and – just before the policeman pulled over – *Try to make a U-turn.* 'No, Bram,' the policeman said. 'You're done.' Then he took the map from the husband. Now he was standing in front of the car with the map spread out on the bonnet. The car door was open. It smelt the way Amsterdam can smell in March with the wind from a certain direction: farmers' spring air. The policeman turned round and peered at a narrow, sunken lane that ran uphill, tufts of grass sticking up through the middle of the asphalt. There was an incredible number of sheep in the field beside the lane. It was damp. The dashboard clock said quarter to one, from which the husband subtracted one hour. He was strangely nervous. It was Boxing Day in Wales and in a quarter of an hour he might be seeing his wife again.

60

He keeps imagining the summit. The way he'd stood there, his breath visible, the Horseshoe, the Irish Sea, the lakes, the gradual slope down to Llanberis, as if the mountain had known all along that they would one day build a railway there. A layer of snow. It was a shame that you were never alone in places like this. The new top station, Hafod Eryri, was closed, sheets of hardboard protecting the large windows, a deep snowdrift against the back wall. It wasn't busy, but the people who were there were almost all talking into mobiles, letting someone know they'd made it to the top. When he got back to where he'd left her – at a run – and didn't find her, he looked over the edge, into the depths, before running on.

But now he's stuck in the cellar of an old pigsty. Without a mobile. Even if he wanted to let someone know he was down below ground level, he couldn't. Standing up straight is impossible. She's laid cushions on the floor, rugs and blankets. It's only after she turns off the light in the pigsty that he uses a match to light a candle. One candle, not both. They're in the necks of two wine bottles. It can't get really dark anyway, not with the house lights on and casting bright rectangles on the lawn. He can see them through the wide, four-inch window. In a plastic bag there's bread and packets of biscuits, butter, a few bananas, a knife, cheese and sliced cold lamb. Is that a joke? He almost smiles. Does she think he's going to eat that? There are three bottles of red wine with screw tops, one bottle of white, seven bottles of water, crisps. A glass and a plate. He hasn't even looked for a second Christmas present. It sounds like she's moving something with the wheelbarrow, footsteps on the crushed slate. The last thing he hears is classical music: the radio must be turned up loud with the window or front door open. Closed again, a bit later. Either that or she's turned the radio off. He doesn't understand, but he's not really surprised. He still pushes hard on the trapdoor and feels the dust drift down on his head. He swears under his breath. '*Sguthan*,' he says, without feeling angry, and '*Iesu Grist*.' He eats and drinks, but not too much. This could last a week. And the likelihood of it being his father who ends up liberating him is something he can't do a thing about. He pulls off his boots and coat and finally removes his hat. He lies down on the cushions without undressing further and pulls the blankets and rugs up over himself. He blows out the candle. He's not cold. The lights are still on in the house. He sees himself on top of Yr Wyddfa, inhaling the biting air, screwing up his eyes in the glare of the snow.

Birds are singing the next morning. With a view of nothing – yes, beams and boards – he could think it's spring. In the course of the night, the cold has risen through the floor after all. He sits up, eats a piece of bread with cheese, drinks some water. And waits. Maybe I got her pregnant, he thinks. He stands up to look out through the window. The grass is damp, and when he looks again a little later, he sees that the sun has advanced quite far. Only now does he notice that she has put the three flowering plants from the kitchen windowsill in front of the cellar window. When he sticks a finger in one of the pots, he feels that the soil is damp.

He still can't work out why he stood there on the lawn like a deer caught in headlights, the headlights of the black pickup parked next to the house. He could just as easily have walked away, climbing back over the wall. Sam had sat trembling against his leg; that was how desperate he was to go to his master. She had given him a sign: incomprehensible, and yet, a sign. Maybe that was why.

He used to be able to stand upright in here, he even had to stretch to look out through the window at his mother and Mrs Evans, sitting on strange chairs in the shade of the alders, next to the stream. It was always cool in the cellar, he didn't understand them staying outside. A couple of glasses of home-made lemonade with ice cubes on a wobbly table. Standing on his toes to look at the women, listening to his mother's voice. Sometimes she'd call out, 'Bradwen!' and Mrs Evans would tell her to leave him in peace, '*Da chi'n gwybod lle mae o.*' And always packing up when his father approached the chairs and table, finished with the sheep and ready to go home, sweat on his nose and brow.

The birds fall silent. Maybe they've figured out it's Boxing Day, or midwinter at least, and not a gorgeous day in spring.

He starts pacing back and forth, bent over in the green-tiled cellar, pressing once more against the trapdoor, which still doesn't give, of course. Dust falls on the concrete steps. He imagines a little boy, a toddler: on a swing or trying to kick a non-cooperative ball. After a while his back starts to hurt and he lies down on the cushions. He's no longer cold. If only Sam was here, even if he did always hold something back, looking over his shoulder, never unconditionally his. He unbuttons his jeans and pulls a blanket over himself.

Hours later, as he's eating some more bread and cheese, he hears a car. Not driving away, but arriving. He keeps still and stops chewing. He'd rather be stuck in a cellar than see his father again this soon. *Be sure to have enough cash for the lost geese.* As if the woman is the fox who's devouring the birds. Car doors open and slam shut, dull and distant, the car hasn't stopped close to the house. Two male voices. They weren't supposed to come until 1 January. Footsteps on the path. They're not speaking Welsh. It sounds like her language: he recognises the harsh gutturals, the strange vowels. He looks around. And again. The flowering plants, the cold lamb, the two wine-bottle candleholders. He puts his boots on and pulls on his beanie. Then he eats another chunk of cheese with a slice of bread, washing it down with a glass of red wine. When he's finished, he starts to bang on the trapdoor.

'Who are you?' one of the men asks. A man with short black hair.

'Bradwen,' he says. 'I'm Bradwen Jones.'

'Where is *Agnes*?' The other man asks that. He's got his lower leg in a cast and is on crutches. He's pronounced the name the Dutch way, at the back of his throat, and Bradwen doesn't understand.

'What?'

'Where is *Agnes*? From Amsterdam?'

'Is that a name?'

'Of course. *Agnes*.'

'There's no *Agnes* here. Who are you?'

The men stay where they are in the doorway, neither of them answering. The boy is standing on the concrete steps. Blinding yellow sunlight shines between their legs, making him raise a hand to shade his eyes.

'No *Agnes*?' says the man with the cast.

'No.'

'What are you doing in there?' The other man says that. The man with hair like his but much shorter.

'She locked me up in here. Emily.'

'Emily?'

'Yes.'

'When?'

'Yesterday afternoon.'

'Where is she?'

'I don't know. Isn't she in the house?'

'No. Why did she lock you up?'

The man with the cast starts talking to the other man in Dutch. He gestures and says the name '*Agnes*' again. The man with black hair keeps his eyes on the boy, even when he's speaking to the other man. He has the wooden slat in one hand. Finally the men step back from the doorway.

'Come,' says the man holding the slat. The boy climbs out of the cellar. The man rests the piece of wood against the wall and goes down the concrete steps. The boy smells him as he passes: strong, fresh aftershave. The man with the cast hobbles over to the house on his crutches. The boy waits until the man has come back up out of the cellar and walks ahead of him to the front door, which is wide open. He looks at the rose arch. The single white rose that was little more than a bud is still a bud, and will probably never open.

In the kitchen both men carry on talking in Dutch as if they've forgotten he's there. Or as if he's irrelevant. The man with the cast is holding Emily Dickinson's *Collected Poems* in one hand. From a lot of incomprehensible sounds, the boy picks out the names 'Emily' and '*Agnes*' and a single '*ach*'. He's standing with his bum against the cooker as if he belongs there. The heat feels good after the cellar. The man keeps talking, laying his hand on a sheet of paper on top of the open map. Next to the paper is the brown felt tip, one of the pens they were supposed to use to plan the garden. The men's bags are on the floor next to the sideboard. The radio is gone, leaving a conspicuous gap. The Christmas-tree lights are on. Now the man picks up a postcard and hands it to the man with black hair. The boy smiles. *Rubbish*, he thinks. *Advertising*. 'Coffee?' he asks, mainly because he feels like a coffee himself.

'When did this card arrive?' the man with the black hair asks.

The boy fills the pot with water and coffee and raises a lid. 'Yesterday.'

'Do they deliver here with Christmas?'

'It was probably already in the letter box. I haven't seen it before.'

'Who are you?'

It's like an interrogation. 'Bradwen Jones.' It feels good to say his own name like that, knowing full well that the man's asking something else. The coffee pot is on the hotplate now, the hottest plate. The boy looks out of the window at the fallen oak. He, too, notices that it's not right to have the slate path running into the lawn like that. There's no reason to it, it doesn't go anywhere. There should be something standing there. He turns round. The man with the cast stares at the postcard, the other man is staring at him again. 'You a cop?' he asks.

'Yes.' And after a short silence, 'You're a smart kid.'

'What's your name?'

'Anton.'

'And him?'

The boy gestures at the man with the cast.

'He's the husband of Agnes. Rutger.'

'Where is she?' Agnes's husband asks. He's talking to the postcard.

The coffee starts to bubble. The boy takes the pot off the heat and gets three cups out of the cupboard.

'What's that note on the front door?' the policeman asks.

'From my father.' The boy doesn't know what else to say about it. He has no idea why his father is coming with an estate agent on 1 January.

'Geese?' the policeman asks.

'There are geese in the field by the drive. Sometimes a

fox takes one.' He puts two cups of coffee on the table, gets the milk out of the fridge and the sugar from the worktop. Agnes's husband looks up. He seems to have thought of something. He stands up and digs a rectangular object out of his bag, wrapped in silver foil. He lays it on the table but doesn't unwrap it. The policeman looks at the boy. The boy looks back, aware of his squint.

Later, he's in the bath. The window is open. The water is hot and smells of Native Herbs. He's sent the Dutchmen to the stone circle. He told them it was a place she liked. 'And if she's not there,' he said, 'there's the reservoir too. A bit further on. She can't have gone far, the car's still here, behind the old pigsty.' He hadn't mentioned any badgers, and no, he wasn't going with them, it was easy enough to find, just follow the path. The policeman had asked him not to leave, as if he was the suspect in a disappearance. He'd laughed briefly in response, which made the policeman smile. They were slow, he'd seen that through the kitchen window, even if the man with the cast was faster than he'd expected. Rutger and Anton. He looks at his penis, which is floating in the water and looks bigger than it is. Pregnant, he thinks. He can't put it out of his head, especially now that he knows there's a husband. And she wanted it; she didn't want to use anything. Where's that radio got to? He closes his eyes and listens to the murmuring of the stream. He weighs up the situation. He could stay. That cop, Anton, wouldn't mind. He opens his eyes and climbs out of the bath. Drying himself off, he sniffs. Emily said she could smell Mrs Evans. He can smell himself and he smells good.

When he opens the study door to get some clean clothes out of his rucksack, he sees that the mattress is gone.

The boy stands at the corner of the house. The big black car the men came in is about fifty yards away. The sun is still shining. A little earlier, from the landing window, he saw the sea glittering. The goose field is in front of him and empty. He starts to walk down the drive, sticking to the field side of the road. Just past the black car, he turns his head because he thinks he's heard trumpets in the murmuring of the stream. Trumpets. The grass on the goose field is very short, the birds have nibbled every blade down to the ground. The boy climbs over the gate and walks slowly, and ever more slowly, towards the goose shelter. The trumpets weren't in the stream, they were inside the shelter. Six months ago the sun was shining too. It was a lot warmer then, the oaks green, the gorse bushes in the sheep field yellow. The grass was growing so fast the geese couldn't keep up with it. He squats down to look in. The planks and chicken wire make it hard to see. He makes out a corner of the mattress; the music is not very loud, but clearly audible. Now he sees that the mattress is lying on a layer of bin bags. The four geese are sitting around the woman. When they notice him, they start to gabble quietly. One goose seems to be resting on her legs and even starts to hiss, as if it's standing guard. He sees something purple too, she has her beanie on. Enough.

He stands up. *A woman with a very nice, purple beanie. She's tired. She didn't make it to the top, but that's not the end of the world. It's Christmas, and time she went home. There is cooking and drinking to be done.* He dredged it up word for word. It was only yesterday after all. *What do you see?* was the simple question, her looking away from him, surly and a little shy, eyes fixed on the water tank. She was indescribably beautiful. He had never seen her like that before. Awesomely beautiful, like a tree or a bush that produces as much blossom or as many flowers as possible the year before it dies. But that was something else he hadn't told her. Emily.

Before climbing back over the gate, he turns round. He looks out over the goose field and the sheep paddocks without any sheep. He thinks of three dead women: two here, one in bed in the house in Llanberis. Just before she died, she said one last thing. He could barely make it out, he was so distracted by his mother's beauty at that moment. 'Go,' she'd said. 'If you want to, or if you have to, go.' Then she'd closed her eyes. He looks at the sky, which is blue. He sees the wooden poles with the electricity cables, gorse bushes, oaks, a few crows, a broken orange tub on the grass, a barbed-wire fence. And, of course, the goose shelter with the music still coming from it. Plenty of shade, even next to the orange tub, a lot more than last summer. That's about it, besides the odd cloud in the distance. Very soft music and the murmur of the stream. He smiles. She hadn't imagined it like this, he thinks. *Let no sunrise' yellow noise / Interrupt this ground.*

The boy packs his rucksack. It doesn't take long; not once has he taken everything out of it. Before leaving the study, he looks at the pile of books on the coffee table and puts

The Wind in the Willows in the top pocket of his rucksack because it has a mole, a toad and a rat on the cover. In the kitchen he looks out of the window. Not a trace of the cop and the husband. He sits down at the table and looks at the sheet of paper. Her handwriting. Her language. The word *bed* stands out in the middle of the first line, *bed met*, but that's about all. The message on the postcard is just two words but equally incomprehensible, *Ik kom*. For the first time he sees her name, it really does say 'Agnes'. The name 'Rutger' is on the card too. He peels the silver foil off the rectangular object. It's a kind of cake with dark brown in it. He gets a knife and cuts a piece. It's delicious; he cuts another. When he's finished, he wraps it back up. He stands up, looks at the Christmas tree and thinks, a lost tree. His gaze passes from the tree to the men's bags, next to the sideboard. He hesitates very briefly, then takes forty pounds from each wallet, even though they both have a lot more in them. He puts Rutger's wallet in Anton's bag and Anton's in Rutger's. With a plastic bag in his hand and the rucksack over one shoulder, he walks out of the house. He changes his mind, sets the rucksack against the wall next to the door, puts the plastic bag on top of it and goes back into the house. Slowly, he starts to strip the Christmas tree, putting the baubles and tinsel and finally the fairy lights in a drawer of the sideboard. After that, he pulls the tree out of the crushed slate and gives the roots a good shake. He carries it outside, down the path that runs into the lawn, fetches the spade from the shed and digs a hole at the end of the new path. Then he puts the tree in the hole and presses down the soil, before returning the spade to the shed. He takes the plastic bag from his rucksack and goes into the cellar one last time. He puts the bread, the cheese and the bananas in the plastic bag, picks up a bottle of water and climbs the concrete steps. He lays the plastic bag on top of his clothes and clicks the top flap of the rucksack shut, loosens a strap on the side and slides the one-and-a-half-litre bottle of water down through it until it comes to rest in a side pocket, after which he carefully tightens the strap. He hoists the rucksack up onto his back, closes the front door like a good boy and walks through the kissing gate in the stone wall.

He crosses the stream. He hasn't decided yet whether to stay on the path or walk parallel to it, on the other side of the thick wooded bank. He knows he has to hike back a full day. He simply took the wrong direction. *Sometimes a day's work is for nothing because it leads nowhere.* He told her that himself weeks ago. The long-distance path has to climb the mountain through Llanberis, giving hikers a choice: on foot or by steam train. And descending from the top of Yr Wyddfa to Rhyd Ddu – with a note that walking the ridge is not without danger – before gradually heading towards the coast. Aberystwyth would be a good ending point. It has a train station. Shrewsbury in under two hours. He should have realised before. This is the wrong side of the mountain.

He looks to the south-west. He still has a couple of hours' light. When he hears voices in the distance, he hesitates, then pushes his way through the wooded bank and squats behind a tree. Someone once told him that nails and hair keep growing after someone dies. How long, he wonders, would an unformed being continue to absorb blood and nutrition? He closes his eyes. He doesn't want to squat still, doing nothing. He wants to walk, to move. Then he sighs and looks at the meadow in front of him, bordered by a thick hedge. As a kid, when he was sitting here and the wind was right, he could hear his mother's and Mrs Evans's voices. He never strayed beyond the range of those voices. In ten or twenty years, not much here will have changed. He doesn't emerge from behind the old holly tree until the men have moved out of earshot. He starts whistling softly.

Spreid dit bed met zorg.
Spreid het ademloos;
Wacht er tot de laatste dag
Luisterrijk en puur.

Het matras zij strak,
't Hoofdeinde rond;
Weer de schelle dageraad
Van deze stille grond.

Emily Dickinson

Emily Dickinson's poetry is quoted from *Collected Poems of Emily Dickinson*, Gramercy Books, New York, 1982.

Use has also been made of *My Wars Are Laid Away in Books – The Life of Emily Dickinson*, Alfred Habegger, The Modern Library, New York, 2002.